"I like a woman with a little mystery."

Anna avoided Marsh's mocking gaze. "You've never forgiven me for something that wasn't even my fault," she said at length.

Marsh shook his head. "I simply assume that whatever you tell me conceals something unspoken."

"You admit that our marriage was a mistake."

"A bargain is a bargain, my love," he said contemptuously. "You've got your job, your independence, your privacy," he said, his hands beginning to caress her. "Why not let yourself go and enjoy the benefits?"

From the depths of her memory the echo of Porter Deman's cruel words confronted her. Anna wanted to push Marsh away and never forgive him for the humiliation he was inflicting upon her. But already her treacherous body was responding to his seductive touch.

WELCOME
TO THE WONDERFUL WORLD
OF *Harlequin Presents*

Interesting, informative and entertaining,
each Harlequin Presents portrays an appealing
and original love story. With a varied array
of settings, we may lure you on an African safari,
to a quaint Welsh village, or an exotic Riviera
location—anywhere and everywhere that adventurous
men and women fall in love.

As publishers of Harlequin Presents, we're
extremely proud of our books. Since 1949,
Harlequin Enterprises has built its publishing
reputation on the solid base of quality and
originality. Our stories are the most popular
paperback romances sold in North America; every
month, eight new titles are released and sold at
nearly every book-selling store in Canada and the
United States.

For a list of all titles currently available,
send your name and address to:

HARLEQUIN READER SERVICE,
(In the U.S.) P.O. Box 52040, Phoenix, AZ 85072-2040
(In Canada) P.O. Box 2800, Postal Station A,
5170 Yonge Street, Willowdale, Ont. M2N 5T5

We sincerely hope you enjoy reading
this Harlequin Presents.

Yours truly,

THE PUBLISHERS
Harlequin Presents

DONNA HUXLEY

intimate

Harlequin Books

TORONTO • NEW YORK • LONDON
AMSTERDAM • PARIS • SYDNEY • HAMBURG
STOCKHOLM • ATHENS • TOKYO • MILAN

Harlequin Presents first edition January 1985
ISBN 0-373-10754-4

Original hardcover edition published in 1984
by Mills & Boon Limited

CHAPTER ONE

PORTER Deman swung his desk chair abruptly to face the young woman before him. A sigh of irritation passed his curled lips.

'You're making this very difficult, Anna,' he said quietly. 'Difficult for yourself.' His cajoling voice was tinged with an undertone of menace which sent a cold chill down Anna's spine.

The springs of his chair groaned quietly as he rocked, his eyes exploring the gentle waves of Anna's auburn hair. The office was silent, its calm disturbed only by the distant thrum of computers printing out sheets of data for waiting secretaries.

Shocked into speechlessness by the insolence of his proposal, Anna Halpern stood livid and trembling with outrage before the man who contemplated her.

'I . . . I can't believe this,' she said finally, her voice threatening to break under the strain of her position. 'I've worked here for four years, and no one has had occasion to complain about me. Quite the contrary, in fact. And now you come along. You've only been here six months, and . . .'

'But I'm here now, aren't I?' he drawled, self-satisfaction glimmering in his cold grey eyes. 'So you'll have to deal with that fact. That's what I've been trying to explain to you for weeks, Anna. But you don't listen, do you?' Again he sighed with feigned exasperation. 'And you see where your obstinacy has got you.'

Anna stared in helpless wonderment at the figure before her. His thinning grey hair immaculately

tonsured so as to conceal the onset of baldness, Porter
Deman was dressed as usual in an obviously expensive
three-piece suit whose fine lines minimised the slight
paunch around his waist. He was the very image of
complacent wealth and influence. His tanned face and
taut skin bespoke long hours spent at a health club in a
deliberate effort to hold off middle age.

The day he had replaced Tom Green as manager of
Anna's research department at N.T.E.L., she had
studied his cold eyes and abrupt manner, and
concluded that he might be a demanding boss. But in
the last month she had realised how catastrophically
she had misjudged him. Ever since the first evening he
had invited her to dinner, in his oddly dictatorial way,
she had begun to fear him. And gradually, as though
inevitably, it had come to this.

'Well?' he asked. 'I'm waiting to hear what you have
to say for yourself.' His lip curled ironically as his eyes
slid over her slender shoulders, coming to rest
languidly on the sleek curve of her breasts under the
silky fabric of her blouse. With studied impudence, he
allowed his stare to stray to her hips, and downward
along the rich line of her thighs, before returning his
gaze to her deep emerald eyes.

'What I have asked of you,' he drawled, 'is not only
quite simple, but also essential to the good working
relationship I must have with you. It is a very
common thing, I can assure you, and not at all worth
staying awake nights over. But, as I've tried to make
you understand, it is necessary.' His eyes bored into
her. '*Necessary*,' he repeated darkly. 'You don't seem
to comprehend the meaning of that word.'

'Necessary,' she retorted, her anger boiling over,
'that I should go to bed with you, simply because I
work under your direction for this company?'

'Now you're putting words in my mouth,' he

corrected with a slight smile. 'It's simply a question of a close personal relationship facilitating an efficient professional one. You state it far too bluntly.'

'That's beside the point,' Anna said firmly, controlling her revulsion with difficulty. 'I know what you mean to say, so there's no sense in denying it.'

'Listen, Anna,' he warned. 'I understand that this all may seem strange to you. It may seem unfamiliar, since you've apparently led a rather sheltered life, but you're simply going to have to wake up to a simple truth. This is,' he said, weighing the words deliberately, 'the way things are done, the way the world is. Now, you'll just have to learn to play the game according to the rules, or get out. I mean what I say, now.' Severity resounded in his deep voice.

She felt herself flush under the insolence of his exploring gaze and the unbearable arrogance of his words.

'I . . . I need this job,' she said quietly, her courage flagging. 'Can't you understand? I can't afford a change of jobs at the moment. I need the income in order to keep financing my sister's education. She doesn't have anyone else. I simply can't afford to be fired, because of your . . .'

He smiled, his eyes glistening dewily with undisguised desire. 'That's exactly my point,' he said. 'You can't afford to go against the grain, so why spite yourself by refusing to do what I ask? If you had had an open mind about things weeks ago, you would never have got yourself into this fix in the first place. Things would have fallen into place, and you wouldn't have had a thing to worry about.'

His tone became more cajoling as he stepped around the desk toward her. 'Think of it this way,' he said. 'I'm not an unattractive man, if I say so myself. I'm not so bad to look at, am I?' He smiled, his finger stroking her hair.

Unnerved by his nearness, Anna stared beyond him at the painting behind his desk.

'Is it so terrible,' he went on, his finger straying gently to her shoulder, its meandering movement leading ever downward, 'to think of sharing a little closeness with me? A little human tenderness?'

Anna shuddered, her nerves crying out in exasperation as the cloying scent of his cologne filled her nostrils. His hands closed around her waist, pressing warmly at the creamy flesh under her skirt.

'That's not so bad, is it?' he whispered, his lips touching the soft hollow of her neck. 'There's no one here. We're alone. Why don't you relax and let yourself go, just this once?'

'Take your hands off me!' Her tense voice resounded warningly.

'Don't destroy yourself,' came his low murmur, 'out of silly stubbornness. Don't be a little fool. I can make you happy.'

Unable to bear his touch an instant longer, she stepped back a pace, her eyes still locked to the meaningless form of the painting on the wall.

She heard a stifled growl of frustration, and felt his hands grasp her purposefully.

'Come on,' he whispered, his lips approaching her own. 'Give me what I want, and I'll take care of you.'

'*No!*' she heard herself cry as the limits of her self-control exploded. The image of her upraised hand seemed a dream before her tormented eyes, but the resounding slap she had planted square in the centre of his cheek was no dream, as the tingling in her palm made perfectly clear.

He stepped back, the growing anger in his cold eyes alloyed by a shadow of genuine shock which gave Anna an inner spark of satisfaction, despite her panic.

He sat down behind the desk, a sore red spot beginning to colour his cheek.

'You shouldn't have done that,' he said. 'You have made a big mistake, young lady.' His eyes glistened with fury.

'You gave me no choice,' Anna said quietly, her hopes collapsing inside her breast. 'I . . . I can't give you what you want. It just isn't in me. You had no right . . .'

'Your explanation comes too late,' he said darkly. 'I'm afraid you've succeeded in destroying what chance remained for you to solve this . . . dilemma.'

'What are you saying?' she asked, the colour leaving her cheeks.

'It's quite simple, Miss Halpern,' he smiled sardonically. 'Your days at N.T.E.L. are numbered. I would say, as a matter of fact, that time has about run out for you. A pity, too. You were so happy here, and your work was appreciated. I shall never understand how certain people can simply throw away what was most important to them.'

'I can report you,' she told him, her thoughts racing to find a weapon she could use against him. 'Sexual harassment is against the law. My work is well known here, and I'll be taken seriously.'

Porter Deman chuckled, shaking his head.

'It's been tried,' he said. 'It never works when the executive involved is important. And I am important, Anna. Far more important to this company than you. I'm sure you're somewhat aware of the lengths your employers went to woo me away from Cambridge Manufacturing. You see, they need me—they need my abilities. And even if your complaints were taken seriously enough to introduce the shadow of a doubt into my colleagues' minds, you would still lose your job. No one likes a troublemaker, Anna.'

'I'll take the chance,' she retorted.

'Go ahead,' he laughed. 'Be my guest. Speak to Charles Robbins, or even the President. Speak to anyone you please. You'll see. You'll be greeted warmly, and you may be lent a sympathetic ear. But in the end, no matter how much your superiors seem to be on your side, you will be politely asked to change your tune or pick up your pink slip. It's a man's world, Anna. If you try to fight it, you'll be wasting your time. But,' he added, a darker look clouding his grey eyes, 'I wouldn't advise that.'

'Why?' she asked, her hatred and contempt threatening to overwhelm her fears.

'In any case, you're through at N.T.E.L. But if you should be so foolish as to cause me any embarrassment, I can assure you I am capable of a revenge that won't end overnight. I can quite easily see to it that you don't work anywhere in this business. Ever.' he smiled smugly. 'Do you follow me?' he asked.

'I'm sure you overrate your influence,' Anna said tartly.

'If I were in your shoes, young lady,' he warned, 'I wouldn't take the chance of finding out.'

Pale with anger and hurt, she stood for a long moment regarding the reclining man behind the desk. His cold, nearly colourless eyes looked out at her like those of a serpent, expressionless and dangerous.

At last she sighed. 'I would like to know,' she said, 'What makes you think you have the right to ruin other people's lives, when they've never done a thing to you, simply because of your pathetic, cheap desires.'

Anger showed in his pupils. 'Get out!' he growled.

'You'd better start seeing to your things—you'll be leaving us soon!'

Anna closed the door quietly behind her, determined not to allow her anguish to attract the attention of the other employees. Porter Deman was left alone in the silence of his office, his chin resting on his hand, his eyes staring before him with an expression of alert intensity. For an instant a look of concern clouded his grey irises. Then he reached for the telephone.

The green eyes which looked out at Anna from the ladies' room mirror had a haunted expression. Even the emerald glow of her irises, normally the most striking feature of her face, seemed blunted by the pressure of the emotions she fought to control. The creamy complexion of her cheeks shone pale under the harsh fluorescent light, making the flowing auburn tresses of her hair seem unusually dark by contrast.

Grateful for the solitude of the empty bathroom, Anna stared intently at her image, struggling to put this morning's events into some sort of perspective.

'Calm down,' she told herself firmly. 'You're all right. Nothing has changed.' Despite his sinister demands and threatening behaviour, Porter Deman was surely bluffing. If he made a serious attempt to have her fired, she would simply defend herself with the truth. Her four years of invaluable service to N.T.E.L. would carry considerable weight in comparison with the unsupported claims of one executive who had joined the company only recently.

And she would not hesitate to tell the whole truth, she resolved. No amount of embarrassment could prevent her from exposing Porter Deman for the contemptible bully he was.

With a rueful smile she thought of the unpredictable and even rash personality which lurked under her calmly efficient exterior. Her stinging slap had surprised her as well as its victim, for in her years at N.T.E.L. she had grown accustomed to keeping her impulsive nature in check, in the interest of her sister's security as well as her own.

In the mirror her admirably sensual figure was highlighted by the silky fabric of her blouse. The gentle swell of her breasts, shaken now by the short, nervous breaths she took, still glimmered with feminine grace. Despite the crawling of her skin, her image remained vibrant and healthy, as though lit from within by the stubbornly independent personality whose wrath Porter Deman had unwittingly tempted.

'Anna,' a voice startled her suddenly, 'are you all right?'

As Debby Johnson's short figure came into view next to her own, Anna realised she must have been too preoccupied to hear the other woman come into the room. Debby's bright brown eyes, normally glinting with mischievous good humour, were clouded by concern as she put a hand on her friend's shoulder.

The sudden appearance of a friendly face was a welcome release after the tension Anna had just experienced, and she smiled gratefully.

'I didn't see you come in,' she said. 'I must have been lost in thought.'

'What did Deman want?' asked Debby, her intuition startling Anna.

'Oh, nothing much,' Anna replied. 'The usual.' She was uncomfortably aware that her flushed cheeks and tense demeanour contradicted her casual words.

'He didn't say anything to upset you, did he?'

'Not particularly,' Anna lied, determined not to refer directly to the disturbing scene that had just taken place. 'Why should he upset me?'

'Listen,' Debby pursued, her brown furrowed in

concentration, 'I don't want to pry, Anna, but I've noticed how edgy you've been every time Deman has shown his face, these past weeks. As a matter of fact, I've been meaning to talk to you about him. He's dangerous.'

'I suppose you're right,' Anna agreed ruefully. 'But he doesn't scare me.'

'That puts you in a league by yourself,' Debby frowned. 'Things haven't been the same around here since Deman showed up. He's got a lot of people pretty frightened.'

'How do you mean?' asked Anna. But her glance at her friend's troubled features left little doubt as to what was in her mind.

'I'll tell you what,' said Debby, 'let's have lunch and talk this over. I have a feeling we can enlighten each other about Porter Deman, and maybe do something about him.'

Anna hesitated, weighing her reluctance to talk about what had happened against the obvious advantage of confiding in someone she could trust.

'All right,' she said at last, reasoning that if Porter Deman had made his threat in earnest, she might soon find herself in desperate need of an ally.

The corridor seemed crowded with secretaries and research personnel as Anna and Debby approached their office. N.T.E.L.'s normally quiet workings often burst into a sudden tumult of activity just before the noon hour, as reports had to be completed, letters signed, and meetings hastily terminated.

'Hey there!' came a familiar voice behind Anna as she passed the elevators.

Turning to see the perpetually laughing face of Bob Samuels, the company's Vice-President in charge of

Research, Anna smiled in greeting. As luck would have it, her momentary inattention to the busy corridor before her sufficed to cause a small collision, and she found herself immobilised by two powerful hands which had closed around her slender arms.

'Sorry,' she heard a deep voice say as she turned to face the tall form she had nearly bumped into. Looking upward past the deep chest at the level of her eyes, she met a dark gaze whose trace of irritation was combined with a glint of amusement.

'Excuse me,' she said, annoyed as much by the mockery in the ebony irises looking down at her as by her own clumsiness, 'I wasn't looking where I was going.'

'My fault,' Bob interrupted, coming to a halt beside her. 'I shouldn't have distracted you, Anna. You haven't met Marsh yet, have you?'

'No,' she answered, darting a diffident smile of inquiry at the stranger who stood before her.

'Well,' Bob laughed, 'this is as good a time as any, since I've caused you to literally bump into each other. Marsh, this is Anna Halpern, one of our research geniuses. Anna, meet Marsh Hamilton. He's working on our contract with Arons and Birnbaum.'

'How do you do, Mr Hamilton,' said Anna, covering her embarrassment with an air of detached politeness.

'Call me Marsh.' The black eyes staring down at her shone with easy familiarity amid the strong lines of a sun-bronzed face. A large hand grasped her own in self-assured friendliness as she noted the dark brow and chiselled jaw which heightened the aura of daunting male strength surrounding Marsh Hamilton.

'Marsh's firm is collaborating with our own legal department on Arons and Birnbaum and some other accounts,' Bob explained, adjusting his glasses with his accustomed nervous energy. 'We're attempting to give him first-class treatment, since he's been kind enough to work with us personally. It's not usual for a partner in the firm to roll up his sleeves, so to speak, and dig into contract details with our young lawyers upstairs.'

'I enjoy it,' said Marsh, his eyes not leaving Anna. 'Gives me a chance to get out of the office. Besides, I think it makes for a better result if your people can connect Feuerbach, Smith and Hamilton with a face.'

The face of Marsh Hamilton would be hard to forget, Anna reflected. Underneath its veneer of calm amiability, one sensed a mixture of sharp determination and unlimited energy which seemed almost reckless. It was the face of a man whose self-confidence had long since triumphed over any obstacles life might have placed in his path.

No wonder, she decided, that he was already a partner in his firm, although the strong lines of his face suggested he was still in his mid-thirties.

'I'm afraid contracts aren't my department,' she said, feeling her senses tingle under the caress of his probing gaze. 'Nevertheless, welcome to N.T.E.L. I hope your work with us goes well.'

'I don't anticipate any problems,' he smiled, not bothering to conceal the frank interest palpable in his expression. 'I expect we'll be seeing each other around, Miss Halpern. Perhaps running into each other would be a better way to put it.'

'I'll try to look where I'm going next time,' Anna laughed a trifle nervously.

'I'd be interested to know more about your research work,' he added. 'It would help me to understand N.T.E.L.'s inner structure.'

'Drop in to our office any time,' she invited. 'Debby

or I would be happy to give you a tour, although you might find it somewhat boring.'

With a sudden glance around her, she realised that the throng of employees crowding the corridor had engulfed Debby. The fascination exerted by Marsh Hamilton's imposing form had made her forget her friend's very existence.

'I'll try to take you up on that,' said Marsh. 'I'm quite sure I wouldn't find it boring.'

'Well,' Anna stammered, unnerved by the enfolding stillness which seemed to immobilise her in his presence, 'goodbye, then. It was nice meeting you.'

'So long,' came his deep voice, its timbre seeming to echo the daunting warmth of his regard.

As she started off down the corridor, Anna could hear Bob Samuels engaging Marsh in conversation. But a sixth sense told her that the stranger's alert glance remained fixed to her receding form, and she could not suppress the disturbing feeling that she was fleeing him toward the safety of her office, like a frightened prey before an aroused predator.

Shaking off the impression with an effort, she pushed open the door and hurried to her desk. This morning's jarring events had distracted her from urgent work awaiting her and the employees working under her supervision. There was no time to lose.

'You can't let him get away with this,' insisted Debby, speaking in low tones so as not to be overheard by the other patrons in the crowded café. 'Can she, Barbara?'

Barbara Moore nodded, her pale blue eyes suffused with sympathy. 'Debby's right, Anna. If someone doesn't stand up to him, there'll be no end to this.'

Anna smiled to acknowledge her friends' support. Debby Johnson and Barbara Moore, themselves best friends and each the other's closest confidante, had made Anna welcome since her first day on the job at N.T.E.L. Their valuable advice on computer programming and the processing of information had made Anna's first months of work a pleasant and exciting experience. And now that Anna had been given greater responsibility and was their office supervisor, Barbara and Debby were far from envious, but more cheerful and supportive than ever.

Unlike her rather plump, impish friend, Barbara was a tall, willowy young woman whose shy demeanour and delicate beauty seemed to bring out the best in all who knew her. She touched Anna's hand concernedly now, as though feeling in her own breast the insult her friend had suffered.

'I'm not sure what I can do,' Anna sighed. 'If Deman isn't bluffing, I'm going to be fired on some pretext or other. But I don't know what it will be, or when it will happen.'

'Look,' said Debby, 'the important thing is that you acted properly. You did the right thing. You have nothing to feel bad about, except the insult of being threatened by that lecher. But now you have to go on doing the right thing. If you don't blow the whistle on this creep, he's going to terrorise every girl in this department, and get away with it. Think of everybody else, Anna.'

'But suppose they don't believe me?' Anna said thoughtfully. 'Deman seemed certain that the executives would take his word over mine.'

'You have to take that chance,' Debby insisted. 'But you may be too worried about it. Nobody around here is more respected than you. I think they'll take your word over his, even if they don't have the guts to fire him.'

'Who should I see?' Anna asked hesitantly.

'Well,' Debby sighed, 'there's no sense going to the

President, he doesn't know you. You can try Chuck Robbins. He's in charge of Personnel, so it's really his problem. Or Bob Samuels: he's a good man, he would be fair. Also, he knows your work.'

'But that would be going outside channels,' Anna objected. 'Bob is in Research. I don't think he would know what to do.'

'I guess you're right,' agreed Debby, darting a glance at Barbara, who nodded uncertainly. 'Try Robbins, then. But don't wait: call him this afternoon. See him right away, if you can. If you tell him that Deman is going to try to get you fired, he'll know what's going on. What do you say?'

Anna sighed, chagrined at the prospect of admitting to an executive she knew only slightly that she had been the victim of harassment. Debby's words rang true, however. Chuck Robbins had the reputation of a demanding but fair boss. Nevertheless, Anna reflected with an involuntary shudder, there might be truth in Porter Deman's words. Perhaps the battle was lost already.

'All right,' she said determinedly. 'It can't do any harm, even if it doesn't do any of us any good—least of all me. Porter Deman promised me I would never find work again if I said anything about this.'

'All the more reason,' insisted Debby, 'to go to Robbins. If he's warned before anything happens, he can use his influence in your behalf. After all, who's to say that Deman won't make good on his threat regardless of what you do? You might as well have someone on your side, Anna. Isn't that right, Barbara?'

Barbara nodded weakly. Since the beginning of the conversation, Anna had noticed, Barbara seemed even more diffident and quiet than usual, and her face bore a pained expression.

'I'm going to have to go,' she said. 'I have a call to make before I go back to work. I'll see you in the office, okay?' She squeezed Anna's hand gently. 'It will work out,' she said. 'You'll see, Anna.'

As she watched Barbara's slender form wending its way among the restaurant's crowded tables, Anna felt a pang of sympathy for her. Barbara was such a sweet, gentle creature. If something like this ever happened to her . . .

All at once the truth glimmered in Anna's mind. Barbara had disappeared through the revolving door. As she turned back to Debby, she could see a look of sad confirmation in the woman's brown eyes.

'You mean . . .?' asked Anna.

'That's right,' said Debby. 'Barbara. Deman has been putting the same number on her that you're getting now. She's such a sweet girl, so vulnerable . . . She's no match for him. She really needs the job. It's an absolute crime!'

Waves of impotent sympathy for Barbara shook Anna, who thought with horror of Porter Deman's cruelty.

'That's why she just left,' Debby continued. 'I knew she wanted me to tell you. Don't you see, Anna? She doesn't have your strength. That's why it would mean a lot to her if you talk to Robbins. You'll be doing it for Barbara as well as for yourself.' Abruptly, she laughed. 'And maybe for me. I know I'm not good-looking, the way you two are—that's why he hasn't bothered me. But if somebody doesn't do something, he'll get around to me eventually. I know his type.' Her face darkened. 'It isn't sex he's after: it's power. He gets his thrills out of terrorising women. The physical part is the least important.'

'All right,' Anna said firmly. 'Before I leave work

today, I'm going to call Chuck Robbins. I'll make an appointment to see him.'

'That's the spirit, Anna,' Debby smiled. 'He'll listen to you, don't worry.'

'Whether he listens to me or not,' Anna frowned, 'he's going to get an idea of what's going on around here.'

But in Debby's eyes there was more sympathy than hope, Anna reflected.

As she walked the short block separating the restaurant from N.T.E.L.'s headquarters, Anna was nearly oblivious to the throng of traffic and pedestrians around her. Chicago's bustling Loop seemed even more vibrant than usual on this crisp autumn day. An El train roared overhead as Anna waited for the light to change. In the distance she could see Lake Michigan, its blue expanse broken by a solitary sail. The enormous public parking lots adjacent to the Art Institute heightened the impression of urban vitality crowded close to the Lake's cold, choppy water.

With a firm smile of determination Anna approached the revolving doors leading to N.T.E.L.'s spacious lobby. Her thoughts absorbed by the turn of events which now menaced the job she had pursued with pleasure for four years, she imagined herself telling the unpleasant truth to a shocked Charles Robbins.

On one hand, Porter Deman's behaviour seemed absurd and almost laughable. One reads about sexual harassment in the newspapers, Anna thought, but when one meets it face to face in the form of an arrogant, ageing executive, it seems both pathetic and ridiculous. Porter Deman had received the brisk slap he richly deserved. Although her meeting with Chuck Robbins would be intensely embarrassing, the ordeal would be well worth her trouble.

On the other hand, she thought with a suppressed shudder, the loss of her job at N.T.E.L. would be a crisis requiring immediate and perhaps desperate action. The slightest gap in her earnings would upset the delicate balance which maintained her own life while paying her sister Sally's college tuition.

Five years ago, when she had first moved to Chicago, life had been far simpler, for she had only herself to consider. She was fresh out of college, and looking for an interesting career. The family was safe and happy in Bloomington, and Sally was a freshman in high school.

Then abruptly, with Dad's crippling heart attack and Mother's illness, life had changed. Anna was still haunted by the memory of the two of them forcing smiles through their pain, and of her mute understanding that the impossible tragedy of losing both parents to incurable disease was actually to befall her. As the medical bills mounted, prompting concerned talks with the family's attorney, Anna realised that she must help Sally accept the inevitability of becoming an orphan at the age of seventeen.

In the fearfully short space of two anguished years, Mother and Dad were both gone. Both their daughters had been forced to grow up quickly—too quickly, in Sally's case, Anna had feared.

But somehow she had managed it. Sally had finished high school with good grades, and since Anna was now a resident of Illinois, she had agreed to attend college in Chicago, where the tuition was mercifully low. The urban university was certainly not the bucolic college campus Anna had wished for her sister, but it was better than nothing at all, and Sally had seemed to honestly want to be near Anna. The two sisters called each other often, and their relationship seemed cemented by the tragic circumstances that had left them alone in life.

Despite the strain on her meagre finances, Anna was delighted to be able to assure Sally of the advanced education she herself had enjoyed under happier conditions. Her salary increases at N.T.E.L. had somehow kept pace with the high cost of living, and in another two years, when Sally was on her own, Anna would be proud to think that her parents' wishes for their younger daughter had come true.

But now the loathsome scheming of Porter Deman threatened to jeopardize everything. Sally held a part-time job already, and could not possibly earn more without sacrificing the precious hours required for her studies. If Anna were to lose her position at N.T.E.L., she would have to find work at a comparable salary without delay.

'It can't happen,' she thought determinedly as the elevator stopped at her floor. 'I won't let it happen.' Whatever Chuck Robbins' attitude might be, she would somehow make him see the truth.

'I told you we'd be running into each other.' A deep voice startled her from her reverie, and she looked up to see Marsh Hamilton standing before her in the carpeted corridor.

'Mr Hamilton!' she exclaimed with a little gasp of surprise. 'I didn't see you. I guess I was lost in thought again. This is turning out to be a busy day.'

'Marsh,' he corrected, his black eyes holding her with their penetrating gaze. 'Remember?'

'Marsh,' she smiled. 'Yes, of course.' Her diffident glance once more encountered the hint of mockery in his expression. But warm friendliness was evident in his relaxed demeanour as he returned her smile.

'To be entirely truthful,' he said, 'I was hoping I'd cross your path again today.'

Still a trifle stunned by his sudden appearance, Anna could think of no response.

'You might be able to help me out with something,' he went on. 'If you'd be willing, that is.'

'Of course,' she smiled, 'if it's in my power—which I doubt. I'm just a small cog around here, you know.'

'I don't feel I quite have a handle on the flow of information within your company,' he told her. 'You seem to me the sort of person who would have a good understanding of it.'

'That's an overstatement,' Anna laughed, doing her best to suppress the tingle of fascination she felt in his tall presence. For the first time she noticed the careless waves of black hair over his tanned face, their expanse accentuating the roguish energy which harmonised mysteriously with his air of taut determination. 'I know where our data comes from, and where we send it, if that's any help. Would you like to see how our office runs?'

'No, I won't interrupt your work,' he answered, 'since you say it's a busy day. How about dinner tonight?'

Taken aback by the abruptness of his invitation, Anna struggled to collect her thoughts.

'This is rather sudden,' she replied weakly. 'Are you sure you wouldn't do better to speak with someone else? I mean, someone in a more responsible position?'

'Positive,' he said simply, his slight smile betokening amusement at her hesitation. 'Eight o'clock?'

'Really, Mr . . .' she began.

'Marsh,' he insisted, his teasing grin widening.

'Marsh, then,' she said, exasperated by his bluntness no less than by the undeniable ferment his powerful presence was creating in her senses. 'I'm afraid I really couldn't make it tonight,' she went on, her thoughts returning to the unpleasant interview she must have with Charles Robbins. Against the background of this morning's events, it seemed essential to maintain an attitude of grim concentration. Marsh Hamilton's disturbing effect on her could hardly contribute to the mood of determination she sought.

'Tomorrow night, then?' he pursued. 'Really, you'd be doing me a favour. Will you be busy?'

'No,' she admitted. 'But are you quite sure . . .?'

'For the second time,' he interrupted, 'yes, I'm sure, Anna. May I call you Anna?'

She nodded in consternation. 'It's awfully nice of you,' she said, 'to invite me . . .'

'It's settled, then,' he concluded simply. 'Eight o'clock?'

'All right,' she gave in. 'Let me give you my address.'

She could feel the caressing warmth of his gaze upon her as she fumbled in her bag for a piece of paper. After hurriedly writing her address, she held it out and watched his large hand cover it.

'It's on the near north side,' she explained.

'I'll find it,' he said without looking at the paper which had disappeared into his palm. 'I'll be looking forward to seeing you.'

With a calm smile he took his leave of her, and she went into her office, still disconcerted by the gamut of emotions she had been through in one short morning. Coming on the heels of the disgust and exasperation occasioned by Porter Deman's threats, Marsh Hamilton's handsome form and obvious interest in her had shocked her senses. But there was no denying the frank attraction she felt in his presence, she reasoned, and no sensible pretext for refusing his invitation.

Perhaps, indeed, things would be straightened out by tomorrow night, and she would be in a more relaxed frame of mind. If, that was, her meeting with

Charles Robbins accomplished its purpose.

With a deep breath she reached for the telephone, hoping that his secretary would be able to fit her in for an appointment as soon as possible.

As though to nip her hopes in the bud, a memo caught her eye on the desk before her, and she returned the receiver to its place without completing the call.

'*Please come to my office tomorrow 10 a.m.*,' the memo read. Charles Robbins' hasty signature was scrawled under the message.

For a long moment Anna sat in silence, regarding the blunt words before her. She had not dealt directly with Charles since a new research assistant had been hired for her department several months ago. In her four years at N.T.E.L. she had never received such a message summoning her to his office.

Suddenly the image of Porter Deman's cold eyes entered her consciousness. Perhaps she had underestimated the immediacy of his threat. Perhaps, after all, he was not bluffing.

CHAPTER TWO

CHARLES ROBBINS' physiognomy had always seemed to Anna the very incarnation of the Middle American man. With his greying hair, his amiably rounded features, and the slight bulge of his midriff, Chuck called up images of lazy Saturday afternoons, noisy children, and a front lawn not yet mowed, because Dad was watching a baseball game after his hard week of work. Indeed, Chuck's friendliness bordered on sheepish diffidence as he reluctantly gave orders to his assistants and secretaries. Although he did his work well, and had dealt with many a delicate crisis in Personnel, the gentle look in his blue eyes always seemed to betoken the secret wish that he were somewhere else, reclining beside a fishing pole by a stream perhaps, or watching from a lazy porch swing as his children played.

But this morning Charles Robbins' apologetic smile was not in evidence as he ushered Anna to the chair before his desk. His expression was pained as he settled himself into his swivel chair and cleared his throat.

'Anna,' he said uncomfortably, 'I wonder if you could tell me whether you've ever had occasion to use our computers on the WR-3-A material.'

'WR-3-A?' Anna repeated in perplexity. 'Isn't that military?'

'It's arms sales and agreements,' he informed her. 'The Middle East, to be exact.'

'No,' she said, wondering what on earth such a subject had to do with her own difficulties. 'Our department hasn't touched a military subject in my four years at N.T.E.L. That would be the fifth floor, if I'm not mistaken—Mr Panariello's department. Why do you ask?'

'You're quite sure,' he insisted uneasily, 'you've had no contact with that material.'

'Absolutely sure,' she answered firmly.

'Well,' he sighed, 'this is very difficult for me, Anna. Very embarrassing. A whole series of print-outs from that file has been found in your desk. So,' he cleared his throat, 'I'm asking you how you think it might have got there.' He hesitated before adding superfluously, 'Series A 16.'

'It's impossible,' Anna responded. 'I don't have any use for that material, nor do I have clearance to pull it in the first place. It couldn't have been in my desk, unless there's some mistake.' Too late, she began to realise the import of Charles Robbins' words.

'Anna,' he sighed, 'this is really very difficult, very painful for me. Please, don't say anything now until I'm finished.' He twisted uncomfortably in his chair. 'N.T.E.L. is, as you know, an information processing company. Our clients confide data in us for analysis, and our job is to advise them on the patterns and implications of the information we study. It is of course essential that the client trust in our absolute confidentiality. Our reputation is based on that trust.'

His gaze was directed through the tinted panes of the windows to the skyscrapers along the horizon. At intervals he darted a glance to Anna's eyes. 'Naturally,' he went on, 'as big as we are, one of our most valued clients is the Federal Government. In order to fulfill our Government contracts, we have to work with classified material, so our personnel has to be organised in terms of security clearance. If an employee is found to have handled material for which he or she was not cleared, that employee has to be let go—immediately. The reputation of the entire company is at stake, of course, so, inhuman as it seems, I must say the rule is necessary.'

He looked at the file on the desk top before him. 'Now,' he went on, 'this material was pulled from the computer under your personal access code. 1289, isn't it?'

Anna nodded, realising what had happened, and that it was impossible to prove her innocence.

'The classification code was punched in, of course, or the computer wouldn't have responded,' he said. 'Although you didn't have clearance for this material, you know the computer well enough to be aware of the various classification codes.' A forced look of anger came over his naturally friendly features. 'I have no choice but to let you go, Anna—I'm sure you realise that. But I know you'll understand how important it is to us to know what motivated your action. Who put you up to it, so to speak. I think,' he added, 'I'm in a position to say that if you give me that information, it will go easier for you.'

Anna sighed. It was obvious what had happened. Porter Deman had simply used her access code to pull the WR-3-A material, had had it printed out, and brought it straight to Charles Robbins.

'May I ask,' she said, 'who discovered this material in my desk? Who brought it to your attention?'

'You know I can't tell you that,' he answered, irritation in his voice. 'Naturally I have to protect the source against possible reprisals. Besides, it doesn't make any difference who found it; what matters is that it was there. Now are you going to tell me why you wanted this file?'

Bitterly, Anna pondered the efficiency of Porter Deman's strategy. There was no way she could defend herself convincingly.

'I never pulled that file,' she said simply. 'I would have no reason to look at it, and I never did look at it. There's either some mistake, or . . . or I don't know what.'

Charles Robbins sighed. Plainly, he had expected just such a denial.

'So,' he said, 'you don't intend to tell me who put you up to this?'

'No one put me up to anything,' she retorted, angered by the tone of his words. 'I've never seen that file.'

'Then we're at a standstill, aren't we?' he said.

Desperately Anna searched her memory of the company's operations to find a way of exposing Porter Deman's treachery. But it was impossible. He had clearly acted immediately, so that she would be accused of a security breach before she had time to report his harassment to Charles Robbins, or anyone else. Now the classified file was a *fait accompli*, and her own explanation of the situation would sound like a desperate and improbable attempt at self-defence.

'I'm afraid,' she said simply, 'I can't enlighten you about this. I've worked for this company for four years, and never had any problems. I know nothing about the file you're talking about. Beyond my own work record and reputation within the company, I can't offer anything to support what I say. It happens to be the truth, however.' Bitterly she heard the hollow ring of her words.

Chuck was staring at her with a perplexed intensity.

'Anna,' he said at last, 'I'm going to have to let you go. You can understand, of course, why that is unavoidable. But in view of your spotless record with the company, and my personal regard for you, I'm going to take a chance. I may regret it, but I can't help believing it's the right thing to do. I'm going to notate this as a termination due to employee incompatibility, in your personnel file. I will not mention the present episode. This will give you the opportunity to find work in this field, or at least in computers. Of course, any mention in your file of a security breach would be disastrous for you.'

She nodded quietly, too hurt and angry to thank him for his magnamity, yet grateful for his gesture.

'But before I do so,' he added, 'and in view of your excellent work for us, I want to give you one last chance to tell me what's behind this business. I'm ready to listen to whatever you have to say.'

Anna sat uncomfortably in the massive leather chair before his desk. What was the point of saying anything? Porter Deman had been diabolically clever.

Nevertheless, the thought of Barbara and Debby, and all the other women who might someday share her unfortunate fate, drove her to speak.

'Mr Robbins,' she began, 'I can see that it's too late for me to defend myself in a believable way, beyond pointing out that everyone at N.T.E.L. knows me well enough to see the . . . absurdity of this accusation. But I'll tell you what I think is behind it, for your own information.'

He regarded her in silence, awaiting her explanation.

'This is embarrassing for me as well,' Anna went on, 'but I'll say it anyway. I was asked by one of our executives to do something improper. Something that didn't have anything to do with the company, but improper in any case. I refused. When I did so, I was told that my days here were numbered. And now, as you can see, I'm being fired.'

'Which executive? What sort of impropriety?' Suspicion vied with acute interest in Charles' troubled eyes.

'I don't feel inclined to mention the person's name,' Anna sighed, 'since I'm leaving you anyway, and since an accusation coming from me obviously wouldn't carry much weight. Perhaps you'd better investigate the situation for yourself.' She took a deep breath. 'The impropriety . . . has to do with the fact that I'm a woman.'

In consternation he turned once more to look at the skyline, his lips pursed, before returning his gaze to her.

'You're talking about harassment,' he said, articulating the words with a grunt of displeasure.

Anna made no response.

'But you won't say who the culprit is.'

'I'd prefer not to.' Despite her determined tone, she felt herself flush in embarrassment.

'When did this ultimatum, as you describe it, take place?' he asked.

'Do you mean . . .?'

'I mean, when were you told you were going to lose your job, as a consequence of not going along with this improper proposal?'

'Yesterday,' Anna replied. 'I had intended to make an appointment with you right away, but I got your memo before I could call your secretary. The . . . situation,' she added, 'had been going on for some time before it reached the point of this threat.'

His eyes were riveted to the file on the desk top before him.

'Anna,' he said, 'nobody likes it when the word harassment rears its ugly head. We know it takes place occasionally, but we don't like to admit that it could happen here.'

'It came as quite a shock to me, too,' Anna said ruefully.

'You're not understanding me,' he frowned. 'Coming as it does on the heels of this very serious security breach, your explanation is not very convincing.'

'I know,' she began. 'I already . . .'

'And there's another thing to consider,' he interrupted, his pained expression betraying the annoyance he felt in his inquisitor's role. 'This file was pulled over a week ago. The employee who brought it to me had hesitated for several days—out of regard for you, I might add, and disbelief—to make its existence known. Now how do you explain that all this started long before the so-called ultimatum you describe?'

In silence Anna weighed the importance of his words. Porter Deman must have found a way to pre-date his pulling of the file from the computer's memory. Anna herself could not imagine a procedure which could override the machine's automatic dating mechanism, but Deman, she knew, was a past master at programming.

On the other hand, she thought, perhaps he had in fact pulled the file days before his final confrontation with her, as a weapon to be kept in reserve against her. Perhaps, in his calculating cruelty, he secreted such evidence against all his prospective victims.

Clearly there was no defence of herself that could compete with the power and expertise of such a twisted mind.

'Well?' Charles Robbins asked.

'I can't explain that,' she replied. 'I know only that for four years I worked here without any problems. Then this business started. When I refused to do what I was asked, I was told I would lose my job. Now it's all over.'

Despite the expression of exasperated stubbornness on his face, Charles seemed to be weighing her words carefully.

'A name would help, Anna,' he said at last with visible discomfort. 'It might help a great deal.'

For a long moment Anna hesitated, her hopeless outrage and involuntary shame threatening to reduce her to silence.

'You suggested,' he prodded, 'that I investigate the situation for myself. Now, a name . . .'

The memory of Barbara Moore's delicate vulnerability decided Anna at last to speak.

'Porter Deman,' she said abruptly. 'And for your information, Mr Robbins, I'm not his only . . . victim.'

Hardly had she begun to pronounce the distasteful syllables when the man before her began to shake his head. With pursed lips and furrowed brow, Charles seemed at once to want to interrupt her and to blot out what he had heard.

'That's going a little far, Anna,' he said reproachfully. 'Porter Deman is a very valuable man to this company. We went to great lengths to acquire his services. He has a spotless reputation in the field, and no one has ever accused him of anything even approaching what you're talking about.'

'I wouldn't know about that,' Anna replied. 'I only know that my troubles started when he joined this company. And as I say, I'm not the only . . .'

'All right,' he cut her off. 'You've said what you wanted to say. And, as I've told you, the situation leaves me no choice but to do what I must do. I'll make good on my promise to keep this problem out of your personnel file. As I see it, nothing remains but to wish you the best of luck in whatever you choose to do.'

'Thank you,' sighed Anna, standing up to leave. Clearly, his haste to end the interview betrayed the incredulity he felt, or wanted to feel. His hands were tied within the company, and they both knew it. Porter Deman had won. There was nothing left but to admit defeat.

'Anna,' he stopped her, 'I really am terribly sorry about this.'

'So am I,' she said, her hand on the doorknob.

'If I can be of any help in any way ...' He had arisen, the friendly contours of his overweight body and rumpled suit contradicting his rigid expression.

'I'll get along,' she responded proudly. 'But there are other women in the company who need your help, Mr Robbins. I'd suggest you give some thought to them.' She closed the door behind her.

Charles Robbins settled exhaustedly into his desk chair. The worst part of this job, he reflected, was letting people go. So embarrassing. So contrary to his helpful nature.

How could she do it? he wondered in perplexity. Of all people, he never would have suspected Anna Halpern of being a security risk. She was the very bedrock of her department, and that was why she had been promoted to supervisor two years ago. The thing strained credulity. Yet there was no denying the evidence.

'Well,' he sighed, 'it's impossible to know what motivates people. She seemed so stable, and now she comes out with this cock-and-bull story ...

'What's the use?' he thought, reaching to touch his intercom button. 'Such a good-looking woman, too. I'll be sorry not to see her around any more.'

'Yes, sir?' squawked his secretary's voice, amplified by the intercom.

'Who's up?' he asked.

'Mrs Adamson is here. Then Mr Foley, then Bob Hamer, and the Miss Moore who called you yesterday.'

'All right,' he said. 'Hold them all. Just a minute.' His finger still pressed against the button, he stared blankly before him. If there was one thing he had learned in business, it was to anticipate the unexpected. At all costs, one must cover all the bases, and spread responsibility evenly. Never sit on top of a situation alone.

'Sir?' Perplexity resounded in the female voice.

What the hell, he decided. Let's be on the safe side.

'Get me Porter Deman,' he said aloud.

Two hours later Anna sat disconsolately at the table in the dining nook of her flat, contemplating the unfamiliarity of the muted midday sounds filtering through the window. Never since she moved in had she been at home on a week day. The unaccustomed atmosphere, combined with the strange faces of the noontime passengers on her Michigan Avenue bus, was intensely disconcerting, and she had to struggle to control the panic that threatened to take possession of her.

Silvery motes of dust floated lazily in the sunlight streaming in the window. The only sound in the room was Anna's turning of the want ads pages, and the quiet friction of lead against paper as she circled the jobs she intended to apply for.

Determined to remain calm and retain her concentration at all costs, she had bought the latest newspapers at the counter in N.T.E.L.'s lobby, glancing for a last time at the banks of shiny elevators and plush expanse of carpet before pushing through the revolving doors to the sunlit street outside.

A few minutes' study had revealed that the *Tribune* and *Sun-Times* contained the same basic listing of available jobs in computer operation and information processing. As soon as she had made herself a light lunch, she would begin making phone calls in preparation for what would undoubtedly be an exhausting siege of interviews.

Only one course of action made sense, she reflected. There was no point in alarming Sally immediately with the news of her firing. Sally would be upset and, in all probability, would generously insist on suspend-

ing her education in order to go to work full-time
herself. But things had not yet reached that extremity.
The severance pay which would arrive from N.T.E.L.
in a matter of days would suffice to finance Anna's
rent and the loan payments for Sally's tuition—for a
few weeks. If Anna could manage somehow to find a
position comparable to her supervisor's job at
N.T.E.L., it might be possible to survive this crisis
without disturbing the routine that had governed the
two sisters' lives for the last two years.

Thank heaven for Charles Robbins' leniency, Anna
thought with a shudder. If he had not decided to leave
her personnel file free of Porter Deman's grotesque
accusation, she would have no chance of finding a
responsible job with a salary sufficient for Sally's
tuition. Even as things stood, though, it was unlikely
that as a new employee somewhere else she could
command the salary she had reached through her pay
raises at N.T.E.L.

'Let's hope for the best,' she said to herself as she
circled another want ad, 'and not get panicky.'
Clinging to what remained of her pride, she recalled
the first weeks after her mother's death, when it had
seemed impossible to earn enough for herself and
Sally at the same time. She had used her wits to cope
with things then, and she would do so now.

A shiver of anger interrupted her disciplined
reasoning as she remembered the cause of her
troubles. She imagined Porter Deman seated comfortably in his office, pursuing his work day as though
nothing had happened, while the woman he had
victimised pored desperately through the want ads in
search of a solution to the crisis he had created. The
thought of his impunity, and of his complacency, was
infuriating. In all probability it would never occur to
him that he had nearly ruined a woman's career. His

only regret would be that he had not succeeded in intimidating her into giving herself to him physically. And now, as he sat in the swivel chair behind his executive desk, he was probably wondering who his next victim might be. Or perhaps deciding to renew his exploitation of someone familiar. Perhaps Barbara . . .

With a shudder Anna suppressed the image of Porter Deman's perverted sensuality and triumphant arrogance. He had won his battle, and was more than welcome to the turf he controlled. She would be far better off somewhere else.

She had not had the courage to discuss the reason for her dismissal with Debby and Barbara before leaving the office this morning. Despite their supportive kindness and questioning looks, she had told them only that the inevitable had happened, and that she needed time to think.

But what was there to think about? Charles Robbins was now in possession of all the information needed to launch an investigation that might expose Porter Deman and exonerate Anna. But his irascible, unwilling demeanour was ample evidence that he had no such intention.

Briefly Anna had toyed with the idea of taking legal action in her own behalf. If N.T.E.L. were forced to justify her termination in a civil suit, the fact of her innocence might somehow be established. Porter Deman's hand must surely be visible behind the denunciation of Anna, even if, in his malicious cleverness, he had had someone else to do his dirty work for him.

On the other hand, she thought resignedly, Porter Deman had anticipated just such a move on her part. Her credibility as a plaintiff would surely be compromised by the classified file planted in her desk.

In order to claim that she was a victim, she would first have to prove she was not a thief and a security risk. And where was she to find the time, not to mention the money, for a legal battle of uncertain outcome? Her memory told her that litigation concerning harassment was a complex, controversial affair in which victimised women were anything but assured of success.

Only one course of action made sense, she told herself. She must find another job immediately, and put the past behind her. Perhaps there was a way to root out and eliminate the evil that Porter Deman had brought to an unsuspecting company—if, that was, the company as a whole was truly innocent of such goings-on—but nothing could avenge his victims. And Anna was among them. There was no changing what had happened; only the future mattered now.

Finding the silence of the flat intolerable, Anna quickly ate a container of yogurt and began telephoning prospective employers in the downtown area. Searching her memory of the Loop's busy streets, she resolved to fill out applications at three locations within walking distance of each other. After boarding the Fullerton Avenue bus, which was sparsely filled with passengers dressed in casual clothes, she began to plan what to say in her interviews.

Of course she would be asked why she had left N.T.E.L. Since Charles Robbins had notated employee incompatibility as the reason for her termination, the best course was to tell a story not far from the truth. Although formerly happy at N.T.E.L., she would say, she found it impossible to work with a new department manager who had been hired six months ago. Her personal file, along with Mr Robbins' written responses to enquiries from prospective employers, would, she hoped, reflect her raises, her increased responsibility, and her good work record.

Four hours later she was aboard her bus once more, in the company of the same preoccupied rush-hour faces she had grown familiar with over four years. Time had permitted only two of the interviews she had planned. As expected, the personnel managers she spoke to seemed impressed by her credentials, but spoke of a lower salary than she had in mind. Nevertheless, they noted, her abilities seemed to promise rapid advancement and an increase in pay. She would be contacted, they claimed, after the weekend—'one way or the other'.

'Which means not at all,' she thought now as the bus stopped in front of her building, 'unless I get the job.' Whoever had said that looking for a job is the hardest job in the world was certainly right, she reflected. The unfamiliarity of offices never before seen, the lengthy applications, the enquiring faces of strangers whose need of help never seemed as urgent as one's own need for a job, made for a profoundly exhausting afternoon.

After a few moments spent poring anew over the newspapers, in search of companies to contact tomorrow, Anna made herself a cup of tea and thought without enthusiasm about what to make for dinner. For a long moment she sat staring blankly at the bland furnishings of the flat, and listening to the city's busy sounds outside. The sinking feeling of alienation brought on by unemployment haunted her as she reflected on the hubbub of activity all around her. Everyone was working, rushing to a job, taking the bus or subway, stopping for lunch at a café, buying new clothes . . . The whole metropolis maintained its tumultuous rhythm through the people it employed.

To be sitting at sixes and sevens, alone in this flat whose perpetually gathering dust and persistent leaking tap were her only companions, seemed intolerably lonely.

Perhaps, she decided, a phone call to Sally would cheer her up. She knew Sally was to leave the city this weekend for a visit to her room-mate's family. Now was as good a time as any to telephone her and enquire casually about her plans, without, of course, mentioning the truth about her own situation. The prospect of hearing a friendly voice, after this day of atrocious solitude, was comforting.

As she reached for the receiver, a thought stole over her mind with such suddenness that her hand stopped in mid-air.

She had forgotten that she was not to be alone tonight after all.

'Marsh Hamilton,' she whispered to herself, cursing her absentmindedness. 'He'll be here at eight o'clock!'

Without a glance at the wall clock in the kitchen she stood up and hurried towards the bathroom. There was ample time for a shower and shampoo before Marsh's arrival, but the idea that she had nearly forgotten all about him lent an involuntary urgency to her movements.

The image of his probing black eyes and calmly determined demeanour followed her into the bedroom, and she shuddered briefly to think of the shocks her nerves had suffered throughout this eventful day. But it was not without a trace of silent expectancy that she dropped her dress into the clothes hamper and began thinking about what she should wear tonight.

She had underestimated the amount of time she would need to get ready, for she had barely finished dressing and brushing her hair when the buzzer sounded.

CHAPTER THREE

Anna glanced for a last time at the swirled mane of her auburn hair in the bedroom mirror before hurrying to the door. The pale green fabric of the dress she had chosen, silky and iridescent in the light of the vanity lamp, was a perfect counterpoint to the creamy complexion surrounding her deep green irises.

She had wondered briefly whether the sleek garment was too revealing for her first private encounter with a man so direct and virile as Marsh Hamilton. But she reflected in all honesty that his dauntingly firm features and hard body had attracted her interest from the outset, and she wanted to look her best for him. Besides, after the depressing events of the last two days her self-respect dictated that she take pride in her healthy beauty.

The door opened to reveal Marsh standing calmly under the pale light of the hallway, the light raincoat over his arm glowing against the dark-toned business suit he wore. Again Anna was astonished by his erect, imposing stature. The outlines of his taut thighs and hard shoulders were visible under the fabric covering them, so that one might mistake him for an athlete dressed in business clothes rather than a professional man.

'So you found me,' she smiled.

'It wasn't difficult. I grew up in this town, so I know the North Side pretty well.' The expression in his dark eyes was unfathomable in the dim light.

'Please come in,' said Anna, standing aside as he entered the living room with long strides.

'Something told me you might wear green,' he said, throwing his coat on a chair and turning to her. For the first time she noticed the small florist's box in his large hand. 'Let's see if this goes with it,' he added, producing a lovely white orchid tinged with blue and green. 'May I?'

'You shouldn't have,' she protested as he pinned the flower to her dress, his long fingers working expertly. 'It's too beautiful.' A breath of the crisp outside air had entered the room with him, and as his clean male scent reached her nostrils she began to feel the potent force of his nearness. Its influence was immediate, and frankly delightful.

'There,' he said, ignoring her words. 'I think it suits you fine. You look beautiful, Anna.' There was blunt admiration in his compliment, and she recognised once more his habit of coming directly to the point.

'You're nice to say so,' she said, trying to forget the electric intimacy of his touch. 'I'm afraid I may have overdressed for our evening.'

'Not at all,' he smiled. 'You'll be the toast of Pierre's. Do you like French food?'

'I love it,' she said, visualising the elegant façade of the legendary establishment in Michigan Avenue's most wealthy block. 'Pierre's will be a new experience for me. My budget has never allowed me to do more than pass it on the bus.'

'Good,' he said, regarding her with undisguised appraisal.

'Perhaps you'd like something to drink?' she asked, blushing slightly under his probing gaze.

'Whatever you're having,' he said.

'Please sit down,' she invited, turning to move towards the kitchen. His tall form seemed to dwarf the small living room as he scanned its furnishings.

'Nice place you have here,' came his deep voice

from behind her as she filled two glasses with ice and opened the whisky bottle she kept on hand for guests.

'Thanks,' she called over her shoulder. 'It's not very elegant, but I like this neighbourhood, and my bus stops right outside the door.'

'I see you take your work seriously,' he remarked, pointing to the computer magazines and journals on the coffee table as she set down the drinks.

She shrugged, not eager to explain the fact that she had lost the job which had caused her to cross his path two days ago. 'I find it interesting,' she contented herself with replying.

'Did you always want to work in computers?' he asked.

'Actually, I majored in Economics in college,' she recalled. 'The computer courses I took were in the nature of a hobby. Then, when I started looking for work here, I sort of fell into the job at N.T.E.L.' Impelled despite herself to change the subject, she asked, 'How about you? Did you always want to be a lawyer?'

'Always,' he said. 'I went through a five-year Law programme here at the University so as to get college over with in a hurry. Then I went to work for the District Attorney, to gain some experience in criminal law. As it turned out, I stayed with them for eight years. Then I joined our firm.'

'Have you switched to corporation law, then?' Anna asked.

'No. I'm working on this N.T.E.L. contract because John Feuerbach is tied up at the moment. Normally I handle the criminal work for the firm. I stay in contact with my old friends from the D.A.'s office, and run into them in court pretty often—on opposing sides, now.' His lips curled in a slight smile, and Anna noticed for the first time that the clean line of his jaw was marked by a tiny scar.

'Looking at this?' he grinned, touching the spot with a long finger. 'That's one of my souvenirs from my days as a prosecutor.'

'What happened?' asked Anna, unable to contain her curiosity.

'Well,' he said, 'some of us used to work closely with the detectives on stake-outs. When you deal with organised crime, you have to be careful of your legal footing. I often helped in arrests. I got this,' he pointed to the scar, 'when one of our targets decided not to go quietly. It was my own fault, really. I should have stayed in the background. But we were outnumbered, and we had to get them while the evidence was right there.'

'And did you?' she asked. 'Get them, I mean.'

'Oh, yes,' he smiled ruefully. 'But they ended up on the street again in no time. That's one reason I finally got sick of being a prosecutor. We got plenty of convictions, but the criminal justice system wasn't equipped to handle organised crime. The big boys could always hide behind plea-bargaining or some other protection. So I decided to go out on my own.'

'Has it been . . . satisfying for you?' asked Anna, a trifle disconcerted by the penetrating eyes that regarded her as he spoke.

'Yes, I'm happy with the law,' he concluded easily. 'It's a complex sort of business, full of ambiguities. But quite often I have the chance to really make a difference for someone who's in trouble. Someone who might have fallen on hard times without my help. What about you?' He changed the subject abruptly.

'Me?' Anna asked hesitantly.

'Is your work satisfying for you?' His black eyes were upon her with their teasing intensity.

All at once she sighed to think that it was impossible

to hold back the truth any longer. She was sitting here with him under false pretences, and the very reason for their dinner together had fallen away with her job itself.

'It was . . . satisfying,' she began uncomfortably.

'What do you mean?'

'I know this is going to sound strange,' she said, forcing a rueful smile. 'I left N.T.E.L. this morning. I'm not working there any more.'

'You're kidding!' Incredulity vied with intent curiosity in his quirked brow and alert eyes.

'I wish I were kidding,' she sighed. 'The fact is, Mr—Marsh—that I'm worth less than nothing to you as a source of information about the way the company works. I suppose I should have thought of a way to inform you of what had happened, so you wouldn't have had to go to the trouble of coming all the way over here. But I was so busy today . . .' She felt her cheeks colour with chagrin.

'What happened?' he asked simply.

'It's . . . it's not something I'd prefer to talk about,' she replied. 'Let's just say it wasn't working out, so now I'm looking for something else.'

'Well,' he smiled, 'the world certainly is a fast-moving place. If I hadn't bumped into you in the corridor at N.T.E.L. and invited you out tonight, I might never have met you at all. I guess I made it in the nick of time.'

Anna had the distinct impression that he was prepared to respect her reticence regarding the loss of her job, and indeed had other things on his mind. But the false position she found herself in was nearly intolerable.

In silence he watched her, as though in speculation as to her inner feelings.

'So you see,' she went on, avoiding his eyes, 'there

isn't really any reason for our meeting. If you'd like to change your mind . . .'

A low, amused laugh escaped his lips.

'Is something funny?' she asked, disturbed by his unflappable calm.

'No,' he said. 'Nothing is funny. I'm laughing at my own luck. If I hadn't encountered you when I did, I wouldn't have known that you existed. Instead, I'm sitting here admiring a beautiful woman who's wearing the orchid I brought her. And in half an hour I'll be the envy of every man in Pierre's dining room.'

Again she felt herself flush as his laughing eyes rested upon her.

'You're sure, then,' she asked, 'that you don't mind . . .?'

'I think we can be honest with each other, Anna,' he smiled. 'I didn't invite you to dinner to discuss something I can easily find out for myself at N.T.E.L. And I'm sure you were, and are, perfectly aware of that fact. I wanted to see you.'

Diffidently Anna glanced at the bronzed skin around his sharply intelligent eyes. The lines of his face and square contour of his jaw were alive with a masculine interest he had no intention of concealing. For an instant she imagined his handsome features drawing close to her, his powerful hands encircling her as he bent to join his lips to her own. But she banished the thought. There was little point in dallying over the sexual charms of a man who might disappear from her life as quickly as he had entered it.

'I ventured to hope that the feeling was mutual,' he went on. 'Perhaps I was premature. That's not a good thing in a lawyer.'

'I'm sure you're a fine lawyer,' Anna admitted, only too aware that the secret recesses of her body had responded tumultuously to his presence even before he had invited her to dinner.

'Enough said,' he laughed, raising his glass. 'Shall we drink to the beginning of a beautiful relationship?'

She joined him in his toast, suppressing as best she could the confusion in her senses. Only this afternoon she had been hurriedly walking the noisy streets of the Loop in a desperate search for a job to replace the one she had lost under such unforgivable circumstances. And now it seemed as though the world were a kaleidoscope which, in a single turn, could throw everything into a completely different position. The memory of N.T.E.L. and her current difficulties was overwhelmed by the bewitching male attractiveness of Marsh Hamilton, who sat before her now like a lithe athlete, poised for any movement the game might require of him. It was difficult to imagine herself feigning invulnerability to his daunting charms, for already an impudent quickening of her traitorous body sent its dangerous thrill through her mind.

As he helped her on with her coat, the light pressure of his strong hands sent quivers of delight along her shoulders and down her back. Indeed, she thought, Marsh Hamilton seemed a man who thought and did as he pleased. He was doubtless in the habit of overwhelming any obstacles that stood between him and his desires. She had to warn herself to be careful in his company.

The shadowed intimacy of the booth Anna found herself in at the unfamiliar restaurant was hardly calculated to decrease her attraction to the compelling form of Marsh Hamilton. His tanned hands seemed particularly dark against the white tablecloth which glowed under the recessed lights, and again Anna had to admire the stunning virility of his long limbs and authoritative demeanour.

'Have you ever tried a *menu dégustation* in a place like this?' he asked.

'I've never been in a place like this,' Anna laughed.

'I think you'll like it,' he smiled. 'It's an assortment of small items, not too overwhelming for the appetite, and it gives the chef a chance to show off his skills. Shall we give it a try?'

Anna nodded happily.

'And a light white wine,' he added. 'That will leave us plenty of room for dessert, which is really an art form here.'

'I don't know whether my waistline will stand it,' she laughed. 'But for Pierre perhaps I'll make an exception.'

'That's the spirit!' he smiled, the teasing glimmer in his dark irises caressing her in the shadows.

Anna was unprepared for the complex and brilliant variety of the dishes brought by the decorous waiter, who faded into the background between courses, returning only to refill their wine glasses. And each surprise experienced by her palate was accompanied by something new to learn about Marsh Hamilton. He spoke of himself with simple directness, revealing the facts of his life in a detached and humorous manner. Clearly the needs of his pride and ambition had long since found satisfaction from his abilities, for there was no trace of egotism or unfulfilled longing in his personality.

His late father, he said, had been a successful small businessman in Chicago until the postwar recession forced him to sell out.

'He was a smart man,' Marsh explained, 'but his excitement over his own products made him forget the hard facts about overhead and taxation in those changing times. The recession took him by surprise and he couldn't pay his debts. He ended up by working the rest of his days for the competitors who bought him out. It was a sad fate for an ambitious fellow like him.'

He shrugged. 'And I'll have to admit,' he added, 'it made its mark on me as well. After what happened to Dad I made up my mind that I would know all the facts before making any decisions in whatever line of work I chose. The law, it turns out, is just the field to keep me on my toes.'

'Why is that?' asked Anna.

'The name of the legal game is research,' he explained. 'A trial lawyer who's worth his salt never asks a question in court without knowing the answer beforehand. He has to realise that his own witnesses are as unpredictable as those of the opposition, and may be hiding any number of embarrassing facts from him. If he doesn't learn to cover the ground thoroughly before going to trial, he's going to find himself losing cases he should have won.'

He laughed. 'But I don't know why I'm telling you all this,' he said. 'You work in research yourself, so I'm sure you know the pitfalls.'

I thought I did, Anna reflected ruefully behind her smile. The confident man beside her was clearly in the habit of reaping triumph from his professional efforts, and was a stranger to the role of victim. Yet his sympathetic demeanour suggested that he understood those who had fallen prey to life's injustices, and had dedicated himself to helping them as best he could.

'Down at our office,' he went on easily, 'they call me No Surprises Hamilton. I'm such a stickler for detail and preparation that the clerks dread working with me!'

'I'm sure they're happy when their efforts help you to win a case,' said Anna.

'I want them to be proud when we win,' he nodded. 'Every case is theirs as much as mine. Some of them see their research as scut work unrelated to the outcome. I try to make them understand that each piece of information they dig up may make the difference between winning and losing. The good young lawyers learn to appreciate that fact in a hurry. The client's whole life may depend on it.'

'The next time I need a lawyer, I'll know where to come,' Anna laughed, realising uncomfortably that even the talents of a Marsh Hamilton might prove unavailing in her present crisis—assuming for the sake of fantasy that she could afford his firm's fees.

'I hope I won't have to wait that long to see you again,' he said, his deep voice enfolding her with its quiet tones. Again she felt the curious power of his gaze. Alive with penetrating insight, it nevertheless rested upon her like a gentle touch, lithe and warm, inspiring her confidence even as it stirred her senses. A stern perfectionist where his work was concerned, Marsh Hamilton had no need to withhold the frank admiration he bestowed upon Anna so naturally.

The impression was heightened by his sympathetic attention to her account of her own past, which culminated in the untimely deaths of her parents and her continuing devotion to Sally. Strangely, Marsh seemed to take for granted the determined strength with which Anna had coped with her situation, as though he already knew her well enough to assume that no crisis could shake her confidence in herself. Retaining his silence regarding the reason why she had left N.T.E.L., he seemed willing to wait for her to discuss it in her own time.

'I have an idea,' he said as Anna sipped the rich

coffee that had brought the meal to a close. 'Let's take a walk outside before we drive back. That way we can work off a little of Pierre's cooking.'

'That's the best idea I've heard all evening,' she laughed. 'The dinner was wonderful—and well worth the diet I'll be going on tomorrow!'

The lights of Michigan Avenue sprang into view with particular gaiety as they stepped out into the brisk autumn air. To the right was the long upward slope leading to the river and the centre of the Loop; to the left the elegant shop-lined blocks adjacent to the Water Tower.

'Ever been to Paris?' asked Marsh, taking her arm as he led her through the shadows of the trees lining the sidewalk.

'No,' Anna smiled. 'I've always wanted to see it.'

'We Chicagoans have always made a lot of noise about Michigan Avenue resembling a Paris boulevard,' he said. 'I never really believed it until I had occasion to go over there on business. But it turns out to be true after all. With these wide sidewalks and trees, and the vista from the river down to the Outer Drive, it really resembles some of the big streets on the Right Bank.' He laughed. 'Of course, the Parisians don't have a big lake right beside the city where they can go sailing or windsurfing whenever they want.'

'I don't imagine they have a Daley Plaza, either,' said Anna, 'with a hundred-foot Picasso sculpture looking down at everyone who passes.'

'Spoken like a true Chicagoan!' he laughed. 'You're probably right. There's no place quite like the Loop on earth. Do you like art?'

'Mmm,' she nodded. 'I often used to take my lunch to the Art Insitute and spend some time there before going back to work. I have a favourite gallery where I sit and restore myself when I'm feeling tired or harassed.'

'Modern?' he asked. 'The one upstairs, with the Matisses, and Picasso's *Mother and Child*?'

'How did you guess?' she laughed.

'You mentioned Picasso before,' he explained, 'and I seem to remember that that particular gallery has quite a few comfortable benches. It's a bright, cheery sort of place, isn't it?'

She nodded, startled by his intuition. In a dauntingly short space of time he was creating the impression of having known her intimately for months or years. The unseen sparks flowing from his strong hand along the flesh of her arm did little to lessen the feeling. Without urgency or undue forwardness, he was somehow opening her to him, dissipating her resistance so that an unspoken inner closeness sprang into life along with her sensual response to his touch. She knew that this intoxicating caress of his voice and eyes might soon be joined by the probing enquiry of his lips and hands, and she had to remind herself that she still did not know him well.

But somehow it did not matter. Her street was dark and sleepy as Marsh pulled the car to the kerb and turned off the engine. Without a word he drew her to his deep chest, his knowing fingers guiding her along the path of her own willingness, and kissed her with an intimacy that stunned her senses.

His lips explored hers softly, their gentleness contradicting the storm of sudden warmth they spread through her slender limbs. The muscular hands covering her back had no need to force her, for her body knew how to mould itself to his own powerful frame in the darkness. With a little shock of delight she felt his earthy male scent suffuse her. The inflaming touch of his body seemed to expand and multiply the already disturbing visual image of his taut attractiveness.

'You have soft skin, Anna,' he whispered, his lips brushing the tender flesh of her neck and earlobe with maddeningly teasing effect. She felt herself begin to strain against him in a daunting flurry of desire, and her eyes closed as his hard man's limbs held her closer still. Astounded to find herself joined so intimately to a stranger who had emerged from nowhere as her personal life was entering a period of painful upset, she nevertheless let herself go to the wild longing which flared in her every nerve.

The heat of his embrace, so direct and authoritative, bespoke his indifference to whatever obstacles might conspire to separate her from his own desire. He seemed to know all he needed to know about her: that she returned his passion and wanted him already. And so it was with relaxed assurance that he released her, and felt her body rest languidly against his own, too faint with pleasure to recede from him.

'There's one thing on my mind,' she heard his deep murmur against the lush mane of her hair.

'Mmm,' she sighed, still absorbed in her fascination. 'What?'

'If you won't be at N.T.E.L. any more, how am I supposed to get through my days there?' She felt his smile in the lips that kissed her forehead. 'It's going to be pretty dull,' he added.

She nodded, pained by the thought of the desperate days of job-hunting that awaited her. The light touch of the hands cradling her shoulders sent waves of lulling warmth through the naked flesh under her dress, making her worries seem curiously remote.

'Well,' he murmured, 'they can't make me work at night, can they?'

'No,' she smiled, her fingers straying absently over

the shirt covering his deep chest. 'They used to make me work at night, but then I was never the partner in a law firm.'

'What will you do now?' he asked.

'Find another job,' she sighed. 'As fast as I can.'

'I imagine you'll be pretty busy,' he remarked, a trace of teasing humour in his voice.

'Probably,' she agreed.

'Not too busy to get to know me a little better,' Marsh said quietly, his hands slipping to her spine to press her closer to him.

Anne could only nod her acquiescence, for the raw eruption in her senses under his knowing touch fairly took her breath away.

'I'll tell you what,' he went on. 'I have to go out of town this weekend on business, but I'll be back on Sunday. How long has it been since you've visited Old Town?'

'A long time, I'm afraid,' she answered, visualising Wells Street and its charming array of shops and cafés. Although the famous area was virtually within walking distance of her flat, her work had prevented her from exploring it for many months.

'Why don't I pick you up Sunday afternoon?' he asked. 'We can take a walk around, perhaps listen to a friend of mine who plays the guitar in a place down there, and have some dinner.'

'It sounds wonderful,' Anna smiled.

'Two o'clock?' The whispered words brushed the soft skin behind her ear like a caress.

'I'll look forward to it.'

A muted inner voice warned that the days ahead would require harsh self-discipline, and that troubling disappointments were probably in store for her. Time was of the essence, and she must allow nothing to disturb her concentration on the business at hand. But as she reclined in the strong arms that held her, as though resting in the quiet eye of the sensual storm that had nearly carried her away only moments ago, she banished all negative thoughts from her mind. Indeed, Marsh Hamilton possessed an invader's power to storm every barrier blocking the path of his desire. In this charmed moment she could only nestle in the bewitching shadow of his strong will. The future would take care of itself. Tonight was hers.

A mile across the dark city the wall clock showed nine-thirty. The office was deserted, except for Joe, the old custodian, who was certainly on another floor.

The bright green glow of the computer display had a festive look under the subdued light. The machine hummed quietly, having received its code, displayed its content, and accepted the change in instructions. Gone for ever was the message it had carried, lost now in a maze of circuitry which was all too capable of forgetting, when told to do so.

A tanned finger touched the keys while a watchful eye verified the appearance of the new text on the display.

'In addition to the security breach, which constituted immediate grounds for dismissal, it is my unfortunate duty to report that this employee offered improper personal favours in exchange for a promise not to terminate or to prosecute. Regrettably, it was not possible for me to establish the circumstances leading up to her improper query of classified computer data, or the identity of the person or persons for whom this material was intended.

'It is with deep regret that I communicate to whom it may concern this unfortunate occurrence . . .'

Signed "Charles Robbins" and pre-dated, the text took its place among the computer's thousands of files.

When requested, it would be printed up by an unsuspecting secretary and sent out along with whatever letter Chuck might have dictated. The only eyes to see it from now on would belong to the anonymous employers who asked for the dossier.

How wonderful a thing a computer can be, when one knows how to use it properly! It accepts instructions docilely, and transmits the desired material with the automatism of a robot. It is a perfect servant.

There is an entire world in those circuits. A world of information, of people, of events at my fingertips. And under my control.

Now she'll know how far my power extends. Now she'll realise how foolhardy she was to tempt my wrath. To think of her confidently writing us down as a reference! Let her wonder, then, when no one will hire her. Let her suffer, and learn her lesson. How many tears will flow, as the weeks and months go by. And I, only I, will know.

Straightening his tie with quiet care, Porter Deman turned off the fluorescent lights, closed the door and moved towards the elevators.

CHAPTER FOUR

THE Art Institute's Modern European gallery was wrapped in its usual silence as Anna sat on a padded bench before her favourite painting. Here and there she could see a determined art student standing near a sculpture, making careful notes on a legal pad for a course paper. Across the large room, a group of schoolchildren sat on the floor in unaccustomed silence as their teacher pointed out the playful intricacies of a huge canvas. A few young couples strolled languidly about the gallery, hand in hand. Two or three solitary figures sat on benches in the hushed, still air, seeming meditatively closed upon themselves among the colourful works of art.

'I wonder if they're like me,' Anna wondered. 'Here because they have nowhere else to go.' Her last interview of the morning having taken her to Monroe Street, she had crossed Michigan Avenue's sunlit, busy expanse to have a light lunch in the Art Institute's cafeteria. And now, with an hour left before her next appointment, she had mounted the two long flights of marble steps to the room whose paintings were like old friends.

Five years ago, having just arrived in Chicago, she had sat excitedly in this quiet atmosphere, sensing underneath its calm the vibrant hubbub of the metropolis outside. When Sally had come to enrol at the university, Anna had brought her here for lunch in the middle of a busy day of shopping and sightseeing. Like her sister before her, Sally had been overwhelmed by the Art Institute's fabulous collection, and had

stared in wonderment at the classic originals whose
reproduced images she had seen in many a book or
magazine.

It was difficult to remain indifferent when one
contemplated the peaked swirls of oil glistening under
the recessed lights on the surface of a world-famous
masterpiece. One felt one could almost see the artist's
hand at work, and feel the touch of his muscular
fingers on the shaft of his brush. And as one scanned
the walls of the galleries, the paintings seemed like
caged animals, barely domesticated by their frames,
each one a vibrant and mysterious world waiting to
lure the spectator's eye inside, to uproot him from his
familiar surroundings and set him down in a strange
landscape filled with people, animals, trees, flowers
from another time and place.

But today it was different. Today even the paintings
seemed infected by the sinking feeling that had taken
possession of Anna. Trapped in their frames under the
artificial light, they hung as though thwarted,
imprisoned on the walls. Even Léger's *Divers on a
Yellow Background*, which she had always preferred
for its humorous tangle of bodies falling chaotically
through a dreamlike space, seemed somehow sad. As
she gazed now at the large canvas, the faces of the
divers looked downright depressed, in spite of their
antic positions.

It was Friday. Nearly eleven days of job-hunting
now lay behind Anna, their morose passage filled with
increasing menace. She was beginning to adjust herself
to the irony of this new routine of living, which
crowded her days with exhausting activity while
seeming to lead nowhere. It was a nightmarish
existence, busy and yet futile. But it was not without
its moments of excitement. For, at intervals, the face
and voice of Marsh Hamilton interrupted the

monotony of her days, promising something finer and more thrilling than the glum misfortune of her present situation.

True to his word, he had returned from his business trip to accompany Anna on a pleasant walk through the Lincoln Park Zoo to Old Town. An autumnal crispness had sparked the air between the North Side's old apartment buildings. Her hand rested warmly in his large palm as he guided her across streets filled with strolling pedestrians unperturbed by the sparse Sunday traffic.

Following Marsh's suggestion, Anna had dressed informally. Feeling relaxed and happy in her sweater and jeans, she glanced with frank admiration at the tall form of her companion. The cut of the leather jacket above his slacks accentuated Marsh's powerfully muscled shoulders and broad back. Entirely at home in the vibrant city of his youth, he seemed at once to dominate its landscape and to draw the essence of its stored energy into his own personality.

The delicious smells emanating from the restaurants along Wells Street were particularly intoxicating after their brisk walk, so they entered a charmingly decorated café that Anna had never noticed before. As they scanned the imaginative menu, the delicate sound of a guitar stole through the room, and she looked up to see a slender blond man, dressed incongruously in a handsome three-piece business suit, tuning his instrument. After a brief moment of quiet concentration, he began to perform classical pieces with amazing facility, a fugitive smile touching his calm features as his long fingers coaxed delicately modulated sounds and moods from the guitar.

'Is that the friend you spoke of?' Anna asked amid the delighted applause that greeted the close of his first recital.

'That's him,' Marsh nodded. 'He works in a dance band during the week, comes here on Sundays, and performs occasionally with classical groups in concerts. I met him a few years ago, when I was still with the D.A. His car had been stolen by a group of professional thieves we were investigating, and by a miracle we got it back for him before they could strip it for the parts. It was the first car he'd ever owned, and he was grateful.'

'He's wonderfully talented,' said Anna. 'The piece he just played sounded so familiar. It reminded me of Mozart.'

'No wonder,' Marsh laughed. 'It's a Mozart piano sonata that he arranged himself for guitar. So you like classical music, do you?'

'Very much. Especially Beethoven, Mozart and Schubert.'

'I'll be damned,' he smiled. 'We have more in common than I thought. Do you get much chance to hear Solti and the Chicago Symphony?'

Anna shook her head. 'I'm afraid the tickets are well beyond my pocketbook. But I buy some of his records.'

'Well, I'll take you to Orchestra Hall some time when Solti is conducting,' he said. 'A girl can't go through life without hearing some live music, good and loud.'

'Oh, but I do,' Anna smiled. 'Right here in Old Town. I see Junior Wells and Buddy Guy, and Muddy Waters . . .'

'You're kidding,' he explained. 'You like Chicago blues?'

'I adore it,' she laughed. 'When the weather is nice, and there's a Sunday afternoon show at one of the clubs here, I sometimes walk over and listen.'

'Alone?' he asked, a wry hint of jealousy in his quirked eyebrow.

'My friend Debby comes along occasionally,' she answered. 'But I've gone alone often enough. Does that surprise you?'

He shook his head. 'There's not much about you that doesn't surprise me,' he laughed. 'Aren't you afraid of a lot of men hitting on you in those blues clubs?'

'Not really,' she said. 'I've found that people come to hear the music. It's quite safe. Besides,' she added, 'I can take care of myself.'

'I'll bet you can,' he said, his eyes appraising her as he took her hand. 'Something tells me you'd be a dangerous adversary if a person were foolish enough to push you too far.'

'Not so dangerous,' she admitted, ruefully recalling her ineffectual attempt to defend herself against the accusation that had cost her her job.

The guitarist had placed his instrument on a tall stool and disappeared through a swinging door as the small spotlight was turned off.

'I'd introduce you to him,' said Marsh with a slight smile, 'but he's very eccentric when he's working. Between sets he does exercises in the back room to calm his nerves. Whenever I come here he sees me and makes believe I'm invisible. We play tennis together downtown sometimes, and then he asks me how I liked his playing. When he's away from his music he's quite relaxed. I'd like to have you meet him some time.'

'I can see that your work brings you into contact with a lot of interesting people,' commented Anna.

'You're telling me,' he replied pointedly, his large hand cradling her slender fingers as his dark eyes caressed her in the shadows.

'I didn't mean me,' she laughed.

'I did,' he insisted with a gentle smile. 'You know,

that independent streak of yours reminds me of the best things about life in this town. It's an unpredictable place, because it's full of talents and personalities from a thousand different places, who all came here for their own reasons. Put them together at close quarters, and the sparks are bound to fly. Exciting things happen. We all talk about Chicago as an industrial crossroads, but to me it's a crossroads of people's destinies.'

His eyes sparkled with sharp introspection as he regarded the lush auburn curls which strayed across the fabric of her sweater.

'Think of it this way, Anna. Five years ago I was the last person in the world to suspect that a beautiful young woman from Bloomington was arriving in Chicago and, by chance, "falling into" a job at N.T.E.L. Wasn't that the expression you used? Time has many surprises in store for us. For the last five years I've been going about my business, never suspecting that my firm would one day do a job for N.T.E.L., and that I would meet that girl from Bloomington only hours before she left the company. If you hadn't bumped into me outside the elevator last week, we wouldn't be sitting here right now. And one day later you wouldn't have been there to bump into me. But you did, and that makes all the difference.'

'I must say I never thought of it quite that way,' Anna admitted.

'Neither did I,' he smiled. 'Until I met you.'

His reasoning, she reflected, had more than a grain of truth. For the cruel fate that had thrown her life into turmoil was inextricably linked with the chain of events that had brought her into contact with the handsome, thoughtful man who regarded her now. But as she returned his smile she had to remind herself that the deep voice which displayed the breadth of his knowledge and curiosity was also a caressing weapon which progressively weakened her resistance to his daunting masculinity. Marsh Hamilton's charms were as varied as his incisive ideas, and their impact seemed to increase with his every word and gesture.

The probingly intimate kiss with which he took his leave of her that night was undeniable proof that there was nothing casual about his interest in her, and that he was well aware of the feelings he had kindled in her in so short a time.

'I'll be through at N.T.E.L. this week,' he said, his long arms locked warmly about her slender waist. 'I'll do the rest of the job at my own office. We're pretty busy at the moment on a number of cases, but I'll make the time to call you. If you don't mind, that is.'

'I'd like that,' she replied, doing her best to conceal the breathless excitement she felt in his embrace.

'You're sure you won't be too busy yourself?' he asked. 'I know you have a tough week coming.'

'I'll make the time to answer the phone,' she teased, her finger grazing the windblown strands of his dark hair.

'That's my girl!' he laughed. The words coiled around her with quietly persuasive force, for already she could imagine herself joined to this attractive stranger by bonds of trust and intimacy. Her future was a mystery whose unknown course Marsh Hamilton seemed determined to alter, and she could see no earthly reason to struggle against him. Indeed, she felt compelled to quell the traitorous longing which inflamed her towards him with heedless abandon at every turn. Her self-respect dictated that she take the time to know him better before investing unrealistic hopes in him.

Such scruples seemed the least of her worries as the days passed. Although she had felt reasonably certain that the new week would bring a telephone call from one of the employees she had seen during her first long days of interviews, Anna searched the want ads for additional jobs she might apply for in the days to come. Waiting by the telephone would be too distressing a business. She felt she had to continue taking action, moving forward, to give herself the very best chance of finding a new job before the money she had earned at N.T.E.L. ran out.

Thus a siege began, marked by a mood of grim determination which was all too frequently interrupted by moments of near-panic. Each morning Anna gathered her courage, dressed warmly, and stepped out into the windy autumn air for another round of applications and interviews. Returning mid-afternoon so as to be at home in case the phone rang, she did her best to remain calm and cheerful. Between trips downstairs to the laundry room, she ironed clothes, dusted tables, vacuumed the floor, trying vainly to prevent her expectant eye from darting to the silent telephone. At last, when the apartment had been cleaned and re-cleaned, the kitchen cupboards reorganised, and her entire wardrobe scrutinised with an eye to what she might wear on her first day in a new job, she admitted defeat and sat down restlessly by the phone.

Surely, if an employer had called while she was out, he would call back late in the afternoon. If the phone did not ring before five o'clock, that could only mean that no one had called all day. Listlessly Anna read magazines, paged through a mail order catalogue in search of a birthday present for Sally, glanced at an old novel from her college days.

Prowling the apartment, she felt like a prisoner of the stubbornly mute telephone. She could neither spend the whole day out looking for jobs, nor remain inside waiting for calls that never came.

Recalling previous job searches, she was uncomfortably certain that a positive response nearly always came within a day or two of the initial interview. After that, one could always be sure that the job had been offered to someone else.

How could it be that the phone had not rung? There were numerous jobs available, and Anna's qualifications were quite impressive. She had a college degree and an excellent work record, including a promotion to office supervisor. Surely each one of the companies she had visited could use her abilities. It didn't make sense. Unless somehow the disaster caused by Porter Deman's treachery had found a way to communicate itself to the employers who queried N.T.E.L. as her reference. But how? Charles Robbins had promised not to place the accusation against Anna in her personal file.

Unless he had lied . . .

'It's impossible,' she shrugged off her fears. 'Chuck doesn't lie. It can't be the file . . .'

By the end of the week the remnants of Anna's optimistic mood had evaporated, and the prospect of the continued search for work seemed a grim ordeal. Before long she would have no choice but to tell Sally her unfortunate news, and journey to the State unemployment office, hoping against hope that she might qualify for benefits despite the ambiguous circumstances surrounding her termination. The thought of the forms she would have to fill out, and the endless waiting, was nothing if not depressing.

Yet as the tension of her job search became more and more painful, another sort of ferment grew with daunting speed within her breast. For Marsh Hamilton did call, as he had promised. The phone rang when night's calming obscurity had settled over the anguish of Anna's hectic day, and she had to conceal

as best she could the happiness that leapt through her
senses as she exchanged friendly greetings with him,
listened to his news, and expressed forced optimism
about her job prospects.

Behind the relaxed humour of his conversation, the
deep tones of his voice seemed to carry the subtle trace
of the heated embrace that had joined him to her days
earlier. His genial words, superficially casual, actually
bespoke the increasing intimacy of their relationship.
Each sound caressed her ear with a delightful
gentleness, and she could feel his lips close to her own
even as they spoke into a receiver miles away.

Despite herself she felt a schoolgirl's furtive
excitement at this marvellous contact at a distance, and
a thrill of discovery at each new thing she learned
about Marsh. Struggling to contain the undercurrent
of eager acceptance that tinged her own responses, she
knew that he heard it nonetheless, and felt herself
quicken in anticipation of the next time she would see
him.

She was not disappointed, for the charmed weekend
that followed seemed to have been taken from an
entirely different life, full of sunshine and unlimited
hope. On Marsh's arm she explored Chinatown, and
tasted the deliciously varied wares at a shabby but
renowned dim-sum parlour whose clientele included
pilgrims from towns many miles distant as well as
local Chinese families. She strolled past the robust,
joking vendors on Maxwell Street, and accepted
Marsh's gift of a colourful scarf whose blue-green
hues took up the deep glow of her emerald eyes. After
a quiet dinner in a charming restaurant nestled in the
busy streets of Uptown, the couple spent the evening
watching a talented theatre company perform experi-
mental plays by local writers.

The city seemed to have come to life under Marsh's

easy, sweeping gaze, and its sidewalks were friendly and familiar under his confident steps. But while the stunning vitality of the urban landscape passed before Anna in a heady panorama, her mind's eye was fixed in fascination on the dark figure of Marsh himself.

Even as he displayed his almost encyclopaedic familiarity with the city's byzantine political and social fabric, he drew her out on her own opinions and experiences, his attentive eyes resting on her in calm concentration as she spoke. In no time, it seemed, she had bared her innermost ideas on people and things to him, and come to know the reflective personality which underlay his boundless confidence in the skills he put at his clients' disposal.

Her second full week of job-hunting was worse if anything than the first, she found herself clinging to her memory of Marsh's last kiss, so soft and intimate, as a lifeline which might blunt the cold menace of her solitary ordeal.

But it was more than a lifeline. The memory clung to her like a bewitching philtre, suffusing her senses by day and haunting her dreams by night. Though her nerves were stretched to their limit in her exasperation over her predicament, a secret yielding stole under her skin at every moment, and when she noticed it she realised that Marsh had not been out of her mind since last she saw him. When she contemplated her tired face in the mirror, the image of his laughing eyes and hard body seemed to look out at her, gently drawing her closer to him, enfolding her in a warm embrace from which all pain was banished.

'Am I falling in love?' she asked herself in amazement, her gaze riveted to the green eyes glowing under the lush curls of her hair.

It could not be. She barely knew Marsh Hamilton, and had no earthly reason to believe her heedless emotions might have their counterpart behind his inscrutable eyes. He was simply a part of this mad maelstrom of events that had upset her existence so suddenly—and nothing more. Later, much later, when life was under control once more, it might be possible to think of matters such as love. But not now.

Yet the taunting question popped ceaselessly into her mind, threatening to eclipse all other thoughts. And she began to fear that where Marsh Hamilton was concerned, she would never be in control of herself.

Now, as she rose from her bench to leave the quiet gallery and hurry through the Loop's busy streets to her next interview, Anna relaxed inwardly, allowing herself to be buoyed by the certainty that Marsh's knock would come at her door tonight, regardless of the day's events. Having teased her with his promise of a surprise for dinner, he had told her he would arrive by six-thirty.

'Thank God it's Friday,' she thought with painful irony as the throng of pedestrians on Michigan Avenue engulfed her. She had worked hard this week, and earned nothing. The absurdity of unemployment seemed every bit as destructive as its financial perils.

'Control yourself,' she thought firmly. 'Be patient. You'll find a job sooner or later.' Resolved to avoid panic at all costs, she hurried towards State Street.

The afternoon's interviews were cast in the same mould as their predecessors. Mr Morgan, the personnel director whose office was Anna's last stop, seemed to be reciting a prepared speech as he repeated words she had been hearing for nearly two weeks.

'I must say that your qualifications are very impressive, Miss Halpern,' he said. 'Most impressive. Of course, we do have to interview some other people

INTIMATE   69

before making a final decision. We'll let you know one
way or the other . . .'

After shaking his hand and expressing her thanks
with as much sincerity as she could muster, Anna
walked to her bus stop with a sense of resignation and
relief. The week was over. Two days of rest were now
to be hers.

Pushing through the front door of her apartment
building at last, she was anxious to take a hot shower
and erase the traces of the day's depressing efforts
before Marsh arrived. She inserted her small key in
the mailbox and saw the door open to reveal an
envelope bearing N.T.E.L.'s logo.

'My severance pay,' she thought. 'So be it.' The last
of her financial resources were now visible. For
another two weeks, or three at most, she could survive
without additional income. After that, her own fate, as
well as Sally's, would be out of her control.

The urgent sounds of the Friday evening rush hour
reverberated outside as Anna sat in her bathrobe
before her mirror and applied a touch of colour to her
cheeks. Feeling refreshed and energetic after her
bracing shower, she began brushing the sleek auburn
tresses which fell in gentle waves over her shoulders.
To her surprise, the face of a vital, healthy young
woman looked out at her from the glass. There was
something virtually festive in the expectant green eyes
and glowing cheeks under her flowing hair. She had to
admit that today's frantic activity had been distinctly
easier to bear after Marsh's call last night. She was
still admired and respected by someone in this large
and lonely city—someone whose irrepressible charm
could not fail to distract her from her nagging
trepidation.

The soft outline of her breasts was palpable under
the sheer fabric of the dress she chose. For an

uncomfortable moment she wondered whether she had unconsciously selected a garment which would show off her femininity too enticingly. As things already stood, she was finding it increasingly difficult to resist the sensual upset that Marsh was so expert in kindling with his every touch.

'I just don't care,' she admitted to herself in all honesty. Come what may, she needed Marsh Hamilton at this crucial moment of her life, and she was willing to run the risk of a painful struggle against his seductive virility for the sake of his welcome support and interest.

A rather urgent knock at the door interrupted her reverie, and she opened it to find Marsh standing in the hallway, his arms full of grocery bags.

'You the lady who ordered the groceries?' he asked playfully.

'Marsh, what have you done?' she exclaimed.

'This is your surprise,' he said. 'And your dinner. I don't think I've taken the trouble yet to inform you of my cooking skills. But now you're going to find out all about them. I'm going to make us a real Cordon Bleu dinner tonight.'

He took off his windbreaker and stood before her in dark slacks which accentuated the taut strength of his thighs, and a handsome turtleneck sweater. The crisp, vibrant coolness of impending autumn seemed to radiate from him as he smiled into her eyes.

'I should have told you not to dress,' he said. 'But I'll confess that I imagined you'd be looking like a million dollars tonight, and I couldn't resist seeing it.'

'That's all right,' she smiled, feeling the appraising penetration of his gaze in all her senses.

'Before I forget,' he said, reaching into one of the bags, 'first things first. If you'll get me a couple of glasses, we can drink this while it's nice and cold.' He produced a bottle of champagne, its chilled glass beaded with drops of condensed moisture from the warm air, and began peeling the foil around the cork.

'Well, don't just stand there, girl,' he ordered happily, seeing her standing before him immobilised more by admiration for his virile self-confidence than by surprise. 'Let's go! It isn't every Friday we toast the end of the week with champagne.'

The cork popped easily under the pressure of his strong fingers, and the effervescent liquid sent sprays of bubbles into the air as Anna held the glasses out to him.

'Now,' he announced, touching his glass to hers, 'this is how we give a lovely lady a first-class evening after a hard working week. Let me see . . .'

Feigning perfectionistic concentration, he reached into the shopping bags and began producing a lush array of good things to eat.

'Caviare to start, with a touch of scallion,' he murmured, waving a packet of green onions at her distractedly. 'Then a seafood cocktail. A few shrimps, a little lobster: nothing extravagant, not too many calories. We don't want to jade the palate, do we? Let's see . . . Oh, yes, Caesar salad. Lots of romaine, not too much anchovy, easy on the tabasco. Where's the steak, now? Ah, yes.'

He glanced critically at her small oven. 'Just as I thought. An old warhorse like that can't broil. I'll pan-broil our entrecôtes with cracked pepper and a nice white wine sauce. Now, what's left?' He peered into the bag. 'Of course: a dash of artichoke heart, a little soupçon of a potato, a stalk of asparagus. And then, to finish, my speciality: profiteroles with chocolate sauce.' He looked up. 'That's what we're saving the calories for. Well, Anna, what do you think?'

She was too touched by his thoughtfulness and

playful humour to do anything more than smile.
Putting down his champagne glass, he stepped to her
side.

'But first,' he said, 'a kiss for the chef. For
inspiration.' The warm wool of his sweater enfolded
her cosily as he put his arms around her. The cool of
the street had left its fugitive trace on his cheek, and
his tender kiss, already probing with daunting power
to waiting embers which sparked within her, seemed
indescribably knowing and intimate. She rested her
head on his shoulder, allowing his physical strength to
support and soothe her as undeniable stirrings of
desire shimmered through her senses. Quietly his
hands stroked her back, her shoulders, banishing
easily the strain that had possessed her for five days.

'No more dallying,' he said, patting her hip and
kissing her forehead. 'Otherwise I'll get distracted and
we'll never have anything to eat.'

His alacrity in the kitchen amazed Anna as he
picked his way with assurance among her dishes and
utensils. Adding the spices he had brought to her own,
he produced a superb meal with a series of laughing
flourishes. His tall, muscular form dwarfed the space
of her tiny kitchen, and Anna could not help admiring
the seemingly inexhaustible resources of his skill and
confidence. For an instant she reflected in involuntary
jealousy on how many other woman he might have
regaled in this charming way before she met him. In
the tight sweater which displayed the depth of his
chest, the broad power of his shoulders, he was
irresistibly attractive, the very figure of the supremely
eligible, brilliant young professional.

The meal passed as though in a pleasant dream,
suffused by the aura of enfolding warmth which
seemed to emanate from Marsh's caressing gaze and
quiet humour. Clearly aware that Anna's week had

been difficult, he was offering her an elaborate respite from her troubles, and she was only too happy to accept. At last, warmed by the wine he had served with dinner, she sat by his side on her couch, watching the delicate ripples on the tawny surface of the tiny glass of brandy he had placed before her.

'You're a wonderful cook,' she complimented him. 'It was awfully nice of you to do this.'

'I had help,' he smiled. 'Every chef needs inspiration. If you don't mind my saying so, Anna, you look more beautiful every time I see you.'

With the same enrapturing power that had bewitched her before, his lips touched her own. His large hand slipped softly across her shoulder to graze her cheek, her hair. A flare of sudden heat, having slept insidiously within her since his telephone call, shot wildly under her skin, leaving her faint with pleasure.

Struggling to control unwilling limbs, she touched his long arm with tender affection.

'I imagine you've had a hard week,' he murmured against her temple. 'Here, put your head in my lap.'

Pliantly she accepted his suggestion. Slipping off her shoes, she lay beside him, feeling his strong fingers run luxuriantly through her hair, with an occasional pause to massage her neck and shoulder.

'That's heavenly,' she smiled, her eyes closed in rapt fascination at his touch. 'But I'm going to shed my hair all over you, like a cat.'

'Never mind,' came his deep voice. 'Just relax.'

His finger grazed her earlobe, her cheek, before returning to the lush swirl of her hair. A great, warm yielding overcame her tired nerves as layers of tension were stripped from her by his caress. Her hand rested quietly on his hard thigh as she lay numb with relaxation under the protection of his presence.

'No jobs yet, I take it.' The stroking tones of his words belied their meaning.

'No offers,' she murmured, gratefully allowing his intoxicating nearness to dim the painful memory he had evoked.

'No offers for a research genius?' he smiled. 'Isn't that what Bob called you? I can't believe it.'

'I guess the job market is tighter than I thought,' she sighed. 'I'll just have to stay with it until I find something.'

'Worried about your sister?'

She nodded.

'I wouldn't, if I were you,' he said. 'Things will work out in time.'

Time, she thought bitterly. *That's what I haven't got enough of.*

'I hope so,' she said aloud.

Again the sliding movement of Marsh's hands forced her worries into remote vagueness. Greedily her body poised itself to his caress, unwilling to let any other impression compete with the pure probing of the fingers which soothed her. Never had the touch of another flesh seemed so magical a balm, so total a remedy. A purring sigh of satisfaction escaped her lips.

'You're right,' he whispered. 'Just like a cat. A big, sleek cat in my lap.'

'Mm-m,' Anna smiled against his thigh.

But his soft rubbing, and the shifting of her limbs on the comfortable cushions, the heat of his thigh against her cheek, were beginning to take on another, subtler rhythm. And before she could consciously notice how strange was this change which took place little by little, and yet all at once a deep quickening in her senses told her that, as surely as relaxation had banished the day's fatigue, desire had come to wash away everything in its path. The muscular caress of Marsh's knowing hands, only a moment ago a quiet stroking which peeled away layers of discomfort, now probed intimately to awaken depths of longing within her.

For a moment his caress, enmeshed in the billowed maze of her hair, continued its languid movement as though unaware of the change that had come over the flesh under it. She lay suspended in her own delight, resting with mute expectation against the hardness of his thigh. But at length, as though in response to an impalpable message radiating from her depths, his hand touched her shoulder, slid easily under her arm to caress her waist, her ribs, the creamy flesh of her hip.

'Did they treat you badly?' he asked quietly.

'Mm-m,' she sighed in rapt contentment, barely able to concentrate on the past which seemed buried by the daunting immediacy of Marsh Hamilton's body and personality. 'Who?'

'N.T.E.L.'

'N.T.E.L. is in my past now,' she murmured, stubbornly determined to solve her own problems without involving him. 'It's well out of my life.'

'So they did treat you badly.' The tender sympathy in his voice harmonised bewitchingly with the ethereal touch of his hands on her slender limbs.

'It doesn't matter,' she insisted pridefully. 'I can take care of myself.'

'I know you can,' he smiled with frank admiration. 'You're pretty tough, aren't you, Anna?'

'When I have to be,' she agreed, unafraid to acknowledge the fiercely independent personality which had allowed her to cope with many a pressing dilemma in recent years. But the thought was banished as she felt herself raised tenderly from her reclining position. All at once it occurred to her that she had merely tasted the fearsome virility of Marsh's hard body.

She knew instantly that her intuition was not wrong, for the kiss that penetrated her now sent a stunning wave of desire through her senses. The fingertips pressed to her spine seemed to burn through the fabric of her dress to the silken nudity underneath. A lithe, goading shudder of pleasure shook her with delicious intensity. The male desire behind his friendly words was aroused in its full force, coiled around her at last, and irresistible.

For a long moment he held her in suspension, his lips and arms joining her to him in paralysing intimacy. The fabric of her dress, loosened by her reclining posture, grazed the gentle swell of her breast, teased the impossibly taut flesh of her nipple, as a powerful hand closed over it. A shimmer of tickling excitement trembled across her stomach, slipping quickly down her thighs so that she stirred against him in a little spasm of delight.

'Damn, but I want you, Anna.' His deep voice penetrated her dizzyingly, forcing her to see in words what was all too palpable under the flesh that strained towards him. She could not yet answer him, for the traitorous response of her body, quickening in his grasp, took her breath away.

Again his lips claimed hers, their searing exploration firing an ache of desire in her depths. She knew that he wanted her to be his now, and his passion might well have carried her away, had he not somehow stemmed its tide and released her. Lying in stunned pleasure against his taut limbs, she was at once grateful for his restraint and unnerved by the seductive power he had so suddenly unleashed.

'I can't stand this any more,' he murmured, a groan

of desire mingling with the sharp determination in his voice. 'Marry me, Anna.'

Her numbed thoughts came to an abrupt halt at his words.

'But . . .' By instinct she made an effort to clear her mind, to find her bearings. But to her surprise, his proposal seemed so self-evident that she could think of no pretext for questioning it.

'Isn't this a bit sudden?' she smiled. 'You hardly know me, Marsh.'

'I know you,' he said simply. 'I know you well enough to want you and need you. I don't have to know any more.'

She had to admit the feeling was mutual, and overwhelming in its hold over her.

'You certainly make up your mind about things quickly,' she said, slipping her hand into his own with quiet tenderness.

'No,' he corrected, 'you're wrong there. I've had days and nights to think about it, but even that amount of time was unnecessary. It's really a question of years, Anna. I've known a lot of women, but inside I've been waiting for you all along. And now here you are, every bit as thoughtful and beautiful—and independent—as I always knew you'd be. I don't need to wait any longer. My mind was made up for me the first time I spoke to you.'

In silence she lay in his arms, bewitched by the strength of his desire no less than by the daunting flare of exultation that leapt within her own breast.

Calmly he stroked her hair, her shoulder, as his words took their effect.

'Of course,' he smiled, 'as I said to you once, a lawyer shouldn't be premature. I've walked into your life at a difficult moment, and I realise that. Perhaps you need a little time to think things over.'

Though she was flattered by his cautious words, Anna could not help feeling that her past life was already a forgotten thing, banished by the excitement which had overcome her. The hard body and caressing voice which enfolded her now were joined to the centre of her own personality in a mysterious, enthralling harmony. She could think of no earthly reason not to throw herself into his embrace, abandon the concerns that had filled her solitary life for so long, and give herself totally to the joy of belonging to him.

'But something tells me I'm not being premature,' he said, reading her thoughts with uncanny precision.

She shook her head in agreement with him and in wonder at the jarring novelty of the situation she found herself in. The next moment could bring her a new life by opening a door whose existence was unknown to her only two weeks ago. In a flash of memory she saw herself walking the corridors of N.T.E.L., taking the bus, paying the interest on the loans she had taken out for Sally's tuition, without a thought for her own future. That life of determined routine was gone now, as was the preoccupied woman who had lived it. In this heady moment, the unforeseen path to a happiness beyond words had opened upon her, and in her heart she had already welcomed it. She wanted this handsome stranger, and somehow knew already that he deserved her trust.

She could not say no to him, and she knew it. To do so would amount to accepting an exile from her very self, which was already bound to Marsh Hamilton by forces she could not oppose.

'Say yes, Anna.' His deep voice probed to the very quick of her, opening her to him with gentle insistence, drawing the words of acceptance inevitably outward, so that they trembled on her lips, waiting to escape her in joyful freedom.

'Marsh . . .' She could hold out no longer. Her moment had come, and she prepared to welcome it.

With a jangling shock the phone suddenly rang across the room, striking her dumb. The ebony irises that held her flicked reluctantly to the instrument.

'You'd better answer it.' A teasing smile spread over Marsh's handsome features. 'I hope whoever it is has a good excuse for interrupting us.'

'It must be Sally,' said Anna, rising to cross the room. 'No one else would call me at this hour.'

Still shaken by the emotions claiming her attention, she picked up the receiver with an uncertain smile.

'Hello?' she said, glancing at Marsh's tall form on the couch.

'Hello, Anna,' came a deep voice. 'Remember me?'

Turning instinctively away from Marsh, she paused for a desperate second before answering.

'What is it?' she asked, searching for words which would conceal the nature of the conversation.

'So you do remember,' said Porter Deman. 'I'm not that easy to forget, am I?' There was a silence over the line as he waited, probably calculating the effect of his words on her. 'There's something important I have to discuss with you,' he said at length. 'Very important— to you, Anna. Perhaps at lunch tomorrow.'

'That's out of the question,' she said coldly. Hadn't he done enough to her? What could he possibly want now? What did he have left to threaten her with?

'Why?' he asked slyly. 'Not working, are you?' His low laugh sent a chill down her spine. 'I mean,' he added with feigned innocence, 'tomorrow is Saturday, isn't it? No one works on Saturday.'

As he paused again, she understood his innuendo.

'Having trouble finding a job?' he asked.

Feeling Marsh's presence behind her, Anna had to fight back the angry words that came to her lips. A muffled chuckle sounded over the line.

'Listen to me, Anna,' he said. 'I can help you, don't you see? Without me, you'll never find work. I'm all you've got. What do you say? Just a little lunch. We'll discuss things. Just a civilised little conversation, that's all I ask. Otherwise . . .'

'Where?' she asked curtly, at once horrified at his reappearance in her life and relieved to know the source of her troubles. She shuddered involuntarily as she listened to his instructions. Without a word, she hung up the phone, made an effort to suppress the torrent of painful thoughts coursing within her, and turned back to Marsh.

'What was that?' he asked, his eyebrow quirked in perplexity.

'Nothing,' she said, forcing a smile.

'Didn't sound like nothing,' he said.

'It was something . . . that doesn't matter,' she said, torn between her desire to put Porter Deman out of her mind and the necessity of explaining away his call. 'It has to do with jobs,' she added weakly. 'Another interview.'

Marsh had not moved. The dark intensity of his gaze seemed to annihilate the breadth of the room as it reached to caress her slender form.

'Come back,' he said.

Without a word Anna crossed the carpet and buried herself in his waiting arms. She could neither conceal her upset nor reveal the reason for it, so she contented herself with clinging to the strength of the man who held her.

'My poor Anna,' he murmured. 'They're making it tough for you, aren't they?'

She nodded, fearful of his sharp intuition. His observation was disturbingly close to the unspeakable truth.

'That was a rude interruption,' he smiled. 'Some people don't have the decency to let a man propose to his girl in peace.'

She smiled, buoyed by his humour and by the comforting warmth of his muscular arms.

'Perhaps it's for the best, though,' he added, rocking her gently as he touched her cheek. 'I was putting quite a rush on you just now, and I really do want you to have a little time to think over what I've asked.'

For an answer she slipped her hand into his own. Though he could not realise it, his suggestion had a special meaning to her. She must confront Porter Deman one last time, and learn the depth of the danger he posed, before burying him in her past, where he belonged.

For over a week he had succeeded in influencing her destiny through his malignant conniving. She could not turn back the clock, but she could at least inform herself as to the precise extent of his power. There must be a way to fight him or, failing that, to elude him.

Regardless of what tomorrow might bring, she reflected, it could not come between her and the bright future that had opened out before her tonight. Porter Deman was an obstacle, and no more. Soon he would be out of the way, and well out of her life.

The strong arms of Marsh Hamilton continued to support her, sending their waves of tingling warmth through her senses. Here with him, she was safe. The power of his own personality gave her courage to face the coming day optimistically. Thank heaven, she thought, that he had chosen this difficult time to cross her path, and perhaps to alter its course for ever.

So she rested calmly in his embrace. But she could not see the quick turning of the wheels in his lawyer's mind.

CHAPTER FIVE

'Sit down, Anna.'

Porter Deman rose from his seat as the maître d'hôtel pulled the table away from the booth. With chagrin, Anna realised she would have to sit in the intimacy of a booth with him instead of across a table.

'Drink?' he asked. A waiter had appeared and stood expectantly before her. She sat in momentary confusion, unable to think of an answer to the question.

'Bring her what I'm having,' said Porter. 'And another for me.'

Silence reigned between them until the waiter returned. Draining his cocktail with satisfaction, Porter accepted its replacement and twisted the glass absently.

'I love a good strong drink in the middle of the day,' he said, his eyes scanning the expensive appointments of the elegant room. 'They make a good dry Martini here. Go ahead, Anna, taste it.'

The bitter, penetrating taste of the gin was particularly unpleasant, since Anna had had nothing to eat all morning. She felt a deep inner coldness which prevented her from taking any pleasure in outward impressions.

'I'm glad you could join me,' he said. 'In this beautiful fall weather, nothing could be nicer than to get out of the house and meet a beautiful woman for lunch.' Seeing that she did not respond, he leaned comfortably against the plush fabric of the booth and gazed knowingly at her. 'Have you been enjoying the weather?' he asked.

She remained stubbornly silent, fighting against the tumult of emotions inside her. Even to speak to him, to answer his casual questions, seemed an unacceptable participation in his sick game. Yet what choice did she have? She must find out what he had up his sleeve.

'I would appreciate your getting to the point,' she said coldly.

'Why, Anna,' he protested with feigned disappointment, 'what's your hurry? Can't a man enjoy your company for a little while, on such a lovely day? This is a fine restaurant. We should be conversing, relaxing, having a good time.'

Anna stared deliberately into the dewy swirl of her Martini. The olive sat at the bottom of the glass like a strange undersea creature, tilting slightly as unseen currents rocked it. For an instant she imagined the tiny fruit growing on a Mediterranean tree under a bright sun, unaware that its destiny was to drown in this alcoholic liquid which was incapable of supporting life.

'Let's get this over with,' she said without looking up.

'Anna, you disappoint me,' he grumbled. 'You're so impatient. Why, one would think you don't even want to be here! That's a shame, because this lunch could be the key to your whole future. You should be grateful to me for arranging it. Yes,' he sighed, 'this could be the beginning of a beautiful friendship.'

'You're not amusing me,' she said quietly.

The waiter was approaching the table again, his dignified demeanour reflecting the grave mission of taking his clients' order.

'I won't be having anyth . . .' Anna began, only too certain that she could not swallow a bite of food in the presence of Porter Deman.

'Bring us both the trout, Charles,' he smiled,

silencing her with a touch of his hand. 'And a bottle of your Macon blanc.'

'Yes, sir,' said the waiter, disappearing silently.

'They do a superb trout here, Anna,' said Porter. 'I know you'll enjoy it. Now, where were we? Oh, yes— the purpose of our little meeting.' He emitted a grunt of concentration on the business at hand.

'I'm a peaceable man, Anna,' he began, 'a friendly man. I can't stand unpleasantness of any kind. Live and let live: that's my motto. It has stood me in good stead in the past, and will, I hope, continue to serve in the future.'

He glanced wryly in her direction. Unable to take her eyes off the glass before her, she sensed the hesitant approach of his tanned hand, and removed her own instantly.

'I'm concerned and disappointed about the discord, the gulf, that has come between us,' he went on. 'When I first saw you, six months ago at N.T.E.L., I said to myself, there's an admirable woman. Not only is she beautiful, but she has such dignity, such obvious self-respect. A man would be privileged to have the friendship of such a person. Yes, indeed, a man would be honoured.'

His grey eyes glittered with undisguised irony in the pale light.

'And, at the risk of flattering myself,' he went on, 'I thought I saw in your eyes the trace, just the soupçon, of a reciprocal interest. Don't deny it, now, Anna. My eyes don't deceive me.' He smiled. 'But that, of course, is nothing to be ashamed of. Can't two working people take a friendly interest in each other?'

How long is he going to beat around the bush? Anna wondered in exasperation. Debby was certainly right: he got his thrills out of toying sadistically with his victims.

'Now,' he was saying, 'everything was going famously, until we had our little . . . misunderstanding. A very unfortunate thing, that. I truly believe that had you not jumped to certain conclusions, without allowing me to explain myself, to explain the sincerity of my position, our problems would have been nipped in the bud.'

Still staring at the drowning olive in her glass, Anna reflected that the gin would probably dry up the last of its vital juices before Porter Deman made his point.

'And that is why,' he said, 'I felt compelled to take desperate measures, so to speak. I simply couldn't let you go away mad, as it were. I felt, and I still feel, that our relationship deserves another chance. I truly admire you, Anna, and I want to express my admiration by doing my level best to make you happy. All I ask from you is a minimum of co-operation.'

Apparently encouraged that she had spoken at all, he patted her hand with proprietorial tenderness before she could withdraw it. Suppressing a shudder of distaste, she joined her hands in her lap and averted her eyes.

'Is it so much to ask,' he sighed, 'that you reconsider a reaction that anyone would call hasty and ill-advised? Really, Anna, you've been entirely too sensitive. All I wanted from you was a little basic human contact, to make the drudgery of work a bit more bearable for both of us. Now, I'm not ashamed to admit that I'm a man who doesn't give up easily. I generally get what I want in life.'

He paused as the waiter brought the wine. 'Good, Charles,' he said, tasting the amber liquid. 'Here, Anna, try some.' He pushed a long-stemmed glass towards her. 'It's a good year.

'Where was I?' he murmured. 'Oh, yes. Now, Anna, I think you've been entirely too prudish about this whole thing. I'm a reasonable man, and not given to holding grudges. That's why I forgave your little . . . outburst, in my office. But don't you understand? I couldn't just leave it at that. I couldn't let our relationship end prematurely, and on such a sour note. That's why I had to do what I did.'

'Namely?' she asked, relieved that he had finally brought his treachery out into the open.

Porter emitted an ambiguous sound, a sort of sheepish giggle tinged with sly menace.

'Well,' he said, 'I don't want to give away a trade secret by going into the details. Let's such say I took advantage of my expertise in the computer field to'—an involuntary chuckle of satisfaction escaped his lips—'to re-program your job search. It was just a little prank, really, quite innocent when you think about it. But don't you see, Anna,' he went on, feigning deep sincerity, 'I had no choice. You gave me no choice. I couldn't allow you to go away full of bitter feelings. I was determined to repair the damage.'

'The damage you yourself caused,' she said bitterly.

'No, my dear,' he retorted. 'The damage *you* caused, through your stubborn, refractory nature. Honestly, Anna, I don't understand how you can refuse the affection of another person, a person who respects you. Are you determined to go through life entirely alone? No man is an island, you know.'

'If I understand you correctly,' Anna pronounced the words carefully, struggling to face him as dispassionately as possible, 'you've compromised me with the employers I've contacted since I left N.T.E.L. Does Chuck Robbins know about this?'

'Of course not,' he answered with wounded dignity. 'This is a private matter, between you and me.'

'So I suppose I won't be able to find a job,' she

murmured, astounded by the malignance of the man beside her.

'Not at all, Anna,' he assured her. 'What's been done can be undone, just like that. With one phone call, I can see that you have a position worthy of your unique . . . gifts.'

'And what do I have to do? Go to bed with you?'

'Anna,' he whispered, glancing concernedly at the nearby tables, 'must you put such a negative construction on things? What am I? Some kind of monster? I have feelings, too, in case that hadn't occurred to you. Now, I simply want you to give our relationship another chance. If you see reason and do as I say, you'll have a job in no time, and a valuable friend in this business. Don't you see what I'm offering you?'

Before he could continue, the waiter appeared. A trout fillet, bathed in white sauce and garnished with an assortment of aesthetically cut vegetables, was placed before Anna.

'Frankly,' sighed Porter as the waiter faded into the shadows, 'I don't see how you can be so severe about all this. You're a young lady who is badly in need of a friend. You've already made one serious mistake in your profession, and it has cost you dearly. You're going to need help from someone in a responsible position, if you expect to find a decent job. Now, I know you have your sister's education at stake. Why don't you think about her for a change, and swallow your silly pride? You need me, and I need you. Don't you see, Anna? We can't do without each other.'

Suddenly the slice of fish before her seemed terribly forlorn and anything but appetising. She understood only too well what Porter Deman was up to. Like any predator, he was tightening the net around his prey,

and gambling that its fear would make it all the more
vulnerable to him. There was no denying that he
possessed the weapons required to instil fear in her, as
he had in other women.

'So it's quite simple, you see,' he said. 'With me,
you have security and, I daresay, happiness. I can
show you a very good time, Anna. I'm sure you know
I mean what I say. On the other hand, without me,
you're simply finished. I don't know how else to put
it. Now what do you say?'

Her courage flagged suddenly as a wave of hopeless
disgust broke over her. There was no point in
threatening to expose this new treachery to Charles
Robbins, or even in doing so without telling Porter.
He would always find a way to destroy her. He had too
much power, too much influence. There was no way
to fight him.

Somehow she would have to find work without
citing N.T.E.L. as a reference. But what if that failed
as well? What if Porter Deman continued pursuing
her, out of sheer perversity, and found ways to make
her lose whatever job she could find? What if he
decided to telephone her again at home, to torment her
at his leisure?

'I'm waiting, Anna,' he said, apparently satisfied
that the impact of his threat was dissipating her
resistance. 'Waiting for your decision,' he added
severely. 'It's either me or . . . nothing.'

Leaving her fish untouched, she folded her napkin
carefully and placed it on the seat beside her. Unaware
of the thought which was taking shape in her mind, he
smiled to see her pick up her large wine glass.

Predators expect their prey to expose its flanks in
terrified flight, she recalled. When, occasionally, the
intended victim turns to face its attacker directly, the
stronger predator may be so taken aback by the

novelty of the situation that it renounces its meal and searches for a more pliant prey.

Porter Deman could indeed hurt her, she decided. But there was one thing he would never accomplish, even if his campaign of terror went on indefinitely. He would not frighten her into submission. She would not allow it.

'As I see it,' he was saying, touching his napkin to his lips, 'your choices have about run out.'

As Anna's slender arm extended towards him, her hand holding the glass of chilled wine, he watched in mute admiration of her finely formed limbs, for he assumed she was merely gesturing to him. Even when the glass began to tip, he remained motionless, the napkin still held to his lips. Only when the cold liquid soaked the unprotected trousers of his costly suit with a wet slapping sound did he realise what had happened.

Looking up in shock from his inundated lap, he saw Anna pose the empty glass on the table before her with calm deliberation.

She was already on her feet as the waiter approached, superfluously intending to pull out the table for her.

'Goodbye, Mr Deman,' she said, striding firmly towards the exit.

'You'll regret this!' she heard his warning voice behind her. But the maître d'hôtel's respectful face occupied her field of vision as he held a large oaken door open for her, and she returned his smile with an even wider one of her own.

The trees lining the street outside wore the first fiery bloom of their autumn foliage under the early afternoon sun. Walking quickly so as to put the greatest distance possible between herself and the scene she had just experienced, Anna turned the corner into Michigan Avenue.

She hesitated in confusion, not sure whether to wait at the nearest bus stop or walk even further away. Unable to make a decision, she wandered towards the Water Tower, wrapping her coat around her against the gathering Chicago wind. Every year at this time the chilled autumn breeze carried a premonitory hint of the savage winter gusts that would soon follow. Anna's empty stomach, fed only by one sip of a Martini, ached with hunger, but she knew her tense emotional state would not allow her to eat. Though she felt weak and chilly, the fresh air seemed to brace her with its energy.

Elegantly dressed men and women passed her, bound for some of the costliest shops on the Avenue. Ahead, the other-worldly splendour of Water Tower Place awaited the scores of customers who would ride the glass-walled elevators to its tiers of boutiques this afternoon.

An older woman stood before the window of a dress shop, clutching the fur collar of her coat to her neck. A young girl, curiously overdressed, strode quickly along the sidewalk, her expensively cut blonde hair flowing in gentle ringlets over her shoulders. A kept woman? Anna wondered. The expensive mistress of a rich man who worked in the city . . .

Yellow taxicabs rolled heavily by, darting between buses whose motors whined angrily each time they lurched into traffic under the weight of their passengers. The Water Tower came into view, a curiously quaint relic among triumphant skyscrapers, its stone walls glowing like adobe under the bright sun. In the distance, the entrance to the Outer Drive swallowed a stream of vehicles which plunged like hurried blood cells through the city's commuter artery.

Doormen tooted their whistles for cabs under the heavy hotel canopies which protected their guests. Before long, powerful heat lamps would be lit under those canvas structures, to offer the hotels' visitors a measure of comfort as they hurried between the revolving doors and the interior of their taxi or limousine. They would be on their way to dinner, to an evening on the town, to Rush Street, Old Town. Excited tourists, lovers perhaps who had their rendezvous in the hotel, or businessmen, they would give the taxi driver an address . . .

Only a week ago, Anna reflected, she had been in this very spot on Marsh Hamilton's arm, listening to him joke affectionately about his native city, and feeling her senses fill to overflowing with his dauntless male strength. It was impossible to spend more than a moment in his company without becoming infected with his cheerful self-confidence. The city stretched before Marsh as a glittering, vibrant place awaiting his initiative and his domination. If he had ever known defeat or frustration, he had long since overwhelmed them through the irresistible force of his determined personality.

With a smile Anna imagined how heartily Marsh would approve her drenching of Porter Deman's perverted hopes. It was too bad, in a way, that she could never permit herself to tell him about it. Her moment of courageous resistance was over now, and she must face its consequences. Her future in her chosen career was a thing of the past. Unless she could find a job quickly in some other field of endeavour, the fragile fabric of her own life, as well as that of Sally, would unravel overnight.

But somehow she felt no desperation. The cold

liquid that had sent such a shock through Porter
Deman's arrogant features seemed also to have taken
the edge off her own anxiety. At least she had acted,
rather than to have futilely consumed her energies in
flight. And she was free to continue taking action, no
matter where it led her.

On Monday, she decided, she would journey to the
Unemployment Office. After applying for benefits,
she would scan the want ads with an open mind.
Somehow she would find a position without citing
N.T.E.L. as a reference. And she would personally
make sure that Sally finished her education—
regardless of the cost to herself.

Sally had suffered more than enough already. She
would never experience that heady, warm feeling of
leaving college for Thanksgiving or Christmas,
boarding the train or bus, and coming home to a
festive house where the family waited to greet her
excitedly, take her bags into her old bedroom,
overwhelm her with questions about school . . . Sally
would never know the thrill of seeing those smiling,
familiar faces waiting at the station, waving, or forcing
back tears as they saw her off for another semester.
Uprooted from the home that no longer existed, she
could only visit her classmates' parents during
vacations.

But she would get her degree, she resolved, without
a single interruption. In no circumstances would she
allow Sally to toil somewhere as a shopgirl or
waitress while her course books sat in useless idleness
on a shelf.

Absorbed by her determined reflections, Anna
forgot both her hunger and her surroundings. She
strolled homeward through Lincoln Park without
noticing the eager shouts of the children who played
their Saturday games on the lawns between tall ranks

of apartment buildings and the deserted beach. Only when Fullerton Avenue came abruptly into view did she realise that she was nearly home. The long walk had scarcely tired her, for the upheaval in her emotions had resolved itself into a virtually festive intensity.

Only one more tree-lined block separated her from the flat she had rented five years ago for its proximity to the bus line leading into the centre of the Loop. She could not predict whether her next job would force her to walk each morning to a more distant stop, or even to move to a less costly neighbourhood. It hardly mattered, she decided. Wherever she had to live, she would make a home for herself. Whatever work she did would still be an occupation. Life might be difficult, but never impossible.

'Nice day for a walk, isn't it?' a deep voice startled her as she approached her building. Disconcerted, she looked up from the sidewalk to see Marsh Hamilton leaning in casual comfort against the door of his car. The clear light of the autumn sun shone with golden warmth on his dark hair and tanned complexion. The dark slacks and windbreaker that clung to his hard limbs made him an indescribably handsome vision against the urban background which framed him.

'Yes, it is lovely out,' she smiled, concealing her surprise unconvincingly as she strode towards him. 'I'm afraid I haven't been paying enough attention to it. I must have been lost in thought.'

'Head in the clouds again?' he laughed. 'I hope you didn't bump into anyone on the street.'

'Not until this moment,' she smiled.

'Good,' he said. 'I'd feel cheated if you bumped into anyone but me.'

She accepted the hands he held out to her and stood before him, bewitched as never before by the probing gaze of the black eyes which held her with their teasing glimmer. He did not move from his relaxed position, but merely regarded her at arms' length, his large palms warming her cold fingers.

'You're chilled,' he observed, apparently unaware of the charged heat already tingling through her at his touch. 'You ought to be careful with this Chicago weather. Even on a nice fall day it will nip you when you're not looking.'

'I'll try to be more careful,' she teased.

'I'm beginning to think you need someone to look after you,' he added, his long fingers cradling her wrists. 'Bumping into strange men in hallways, going out in cold weather without enough warm clothing . . . You're a woman who needs watching.'

'Perhaps you're right there,' she said, recalling her uncertain attempts to deal with the jarring events of the past two weeks. 'Perhaps I should . . .'

But her words trailed into silence as his hand, having adjusted a strand of her windblown hair, caressed her cheek with lulling tenderness. Her eyes half-closed in pleasure, she stood transfixed by the seductive power of his nearness.

'I thought you were working today,' she said at last, regarding him curiously.

'I was,' he smiled. 'But I'm not any more.'

'I thought you said your partners were . . .' she began.

'Busy?' he interrupted. 'Yes, we're busy. On the other hand, we're always busy. I was looking out my office window at this beautiful sun, and I suddenly had a wonderful idea. I thought I'd check it out with you before putting it into action.'

'Really?' she joked, hoping her banter would disguise the sensual flare his warm hands were kindling under her skin.

'Here's my idea,' he began. 'I happen to know a beautiful lake in northern Wisconsin. It has the clearest water in the whole state, and it's surrounded by thick woods. Birch, maple, oak ... a little of everything. Since it's up north, the leaves naturally turn earlier in the fall, so that on a weekend like this it would be quite a showplace. There are lots of trails to walk in the woods, and a person can go canoeing or fishing or whatever else he wants to do around a lake.'

The black depths of his eyes, tinged with enigmatic merriment, came closer as his arms slipped around her waist.

'And, as luck would have it,' he went on, 'there's an inn there. A very pretty colonial place, with nice sitting rooms and quilted comforters on the beds, and no television, and old faded landscapes on the walls, and a dining room with a huge fireplace. It can be quite busy there in the summer, but today it will be nearly deserted. The owner and his wife are friends of mine. They enjoy running the place, and they both have a lot of personality. Of course, they're not at all pushy. They would welcome us warmly, and then fade into the background so as to respect our privacy. Shall I go on?'

Anna nodded, intoxicated by the tale of bucolic peace he was spinning, and reluctant to stop him.

'It's quite simple,' he smiled, caressing her waist with quiet intimacy. 'You and I would make a couple of stops here in town, just to get ourselves ready, and then we would drive north in my car. It would take a while to get up there, even through Saturday traffic, and it would be dark by the time we arrived. But the fire would be burning, and the lights would be on in the lobby behind the veranda, and we'd have a nice hot drink to warm us up. Then, tomorrow morning, we'd have one of Elvira's special breakfasts before taking a long, relaxing walk around the lake. Before you knew it, we'd have the city's noise out of our systems.'

'You paint an awfully pretty picture,' she sighed, already beginning to count the reasons why it could never become a reality.

'I haven't finished,' he said. 'My partners in the firm owe me more than a few favours by now, so I'm sure they would look the other way if we made it a very long weekend. Since you're not working, it would be convenient for you, and of course it would be just the tonic I need. I haven't bothered to take a vacation in a long time, since I had no interest in relaxing somewhere alone. But now I would be with you, Anna, and I doubt that I would take much notice of the leaves or the lake or the inn. I'd concentrate on being the happiest man on earth.

'Of course,' he added with feigned concern, 'the whole thing depends to some extent on your sister. Is she in town this weekend?'

'Yes, I think so,' said Anna. 'But what does Sally have to do with this?'

'Well,' he said, his slow smile widening, 'you wouldn't want to get married without telling your sister, would you? She'd feel slighted if she missed your wedding this afternoon, don't you think?'

'Marsh!' Anna was too overwhelmed by the boldness of his proposal to think of an immediate response.

'Judge Bardwell is an old friend of mine,' he went on with unflappable calm. 'He'd be available to perform a quiet ceremony for us. I'd grab a witness from somewhere, we'd pick up Sally, and then drop her at her apartment on our way out of town. We'd have our time together up at the lake, come back next

Say Hello to Yesterday
Holly Weston had done it
all alone.

She had raised her small son and
worked her way up to features
writer for a major newspaper. Still
the bitterness of the the past
seven years lingered.

She had been very young when
she married Nick Falconer—but
old enough to lose her heart
completely when he left. Despite
her success in her new life, her old
one haunted her.

But it was over and done with—
until an assignment in Greece
brought her face to face with
Nick, and all she was trying to
forget. . . .

Time of the Temptress
The game must be played
his way!

Rebellion against a cushioned,
controlled life had landed Eve
Tarrant in Africa. Now only the
tough mercenary Wade O'Mara
stood between her and possible
death in the wild, revolution-torn
jungle.

But the real danger was Wade
himself—he had made Eve
aware of herself as a woman.

"I saved your neck, so you feel
you owe me something," Wade
said. "But you don't owe me a
thing, Eve. Get away from me."
She knew she could make him
lose his head if she tried. But that
wouldn't solve anything. . . .

**Your
Romantic
Adventure
Starts
Here.**

Born Out of Love
It had to be coincidence!

Charlotte stared at the man
through a mist of confusion. It
was Logan. An older Logan, of
course, but unmistakably the
man who had ravaged her
emotions and then abandoned
her all those years ago.

She ought to feel angry. She
ought to feel resentful and
cheated. Instead, she was
apprehensive—terrified at the
complications he could create.

"We are not through, Charlotte,"
he told her flatly. "I sometimes
think we haven't even begun."

Man's World
Kate was finished with
love for good.

Kate's new boss, features editor
Eliot Holman, might have devas-
tating charms—but Kate couldn't
care less, even if it was obvious
that he was interested in her.

Everyone, including Eliot, thought
Kate was grieving over the loss of
her husband, Toby. She kept it a
carefully guarded secret just how
cruelly Toby had treated her and
how terrified she was of trusting
men again.

But Eliot refused to leave her
alone, which only served to infuri-
ate her. He was no different from
any other man. . . or was he?

These FOUR free Harlequin Presents novels allow you to enter the world of romance, love and desire. As a member of the Harlequin Home Subscription Plan, you can continue to experience all the moods of love. You'll be inspired by moments so real...so moving...you won't want them to end. So start your own Harlequin Presents adventure by returning the reply card below. DO IT TODAY!

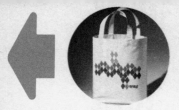

EXTRA BONUS
MAIL YOUR ORDER
TODAY AND GET A
FREE TOTE BAG
FROM HARLEQUIN.

week, move your things over to my place, and live happily ever after.'

'Marsh, I . . .'

'After a while,' he interrupted, 'we'd move out of my apartment and into a house. We'd need more room, of course, in order to start a family. How many children would you like, Anna? Do you prefer boys or girls? Personally, I have an open mind on the subject . . .'

With a furtive glance down the quiet sidewalk, he had drawn her closer to him, and she felt the warmth of his desire add itself to the power of his will in a convincing combination.

'You've thought of everything,' she murmured against his chest.

'I think so,' he agreed. 'We'd help Sally finish college, and of course money would be no problem, since her expenses don't amount to much. In return, she'd babysit for us, I imagine. At some point you might decide to go back to work, if that's what you wanted—but you'd need maternity leave. Yes, Anna, I think I've thought of everything. As I say,' he smiled, 'it seems to me a workable plan. With one proviso.'

'And what is that?' she asked, returning the impassioned gaze of the ebony eyes that held her.

'Do you love me?' he asked.

With a grateful sigh she spoke words that had clamoured to escape her lips long before this moment.

'Yes, Marsh, I love you.'

'And I love you,' he whispered, holding her close to him. 'Shall we give up delaying the inevitable, then?'

For an answer she pressed herself to his hard body as the truth of his words came home to her. The cruel phone call that had prevented her from responding to his proposal last night was no more than a brief delay imposed upon a process which had been gaining momentum since the moment she met Marsh Hamilton.

'You're sure,' she smiled, 'that you want to saddle yourself with someone who has no job, no prospects . . .'

'Oh, you'll have a job, all right,' he laughed. 'You'll have your hands full with me, Anna. And your future will be our future.'

Something of his dauntless, cheerful confidence seemed to spread through her own depths as he held her close. And she knew that it had been so days earlier. Though she had struggled alone with her recent difficulties, she could not suppress the intuition that Marsh was somehow involved in her efforts, somehow supporting her from a distance. In her bitter passage from interview to interview, her blunt revelation of the truth to Charles Robbins, and even her blithe drowning of Porter Deman's lingering hopes, she had gathered strength from the bright image of the man who had crossed her path so recently.

Perhaps, in a mysterious way, she had already been looking back on these challenges from the vantage point of her happy future with him. Perhaps she had coped with them so fearlessly because she knew that the solitary existence they menaced was about to be eclipsed by a new life of unlimited promise.

'What do you say?' he asked. 'All we have to do is cross this sidewalk, go up those old stairs of yours, call your sister, and pack a bag. Then the future is ours.'

Anna felt herself turn to lead him into the shadows of her home. His strong arm rested on her shoulder like a steadfast beacon which freed her from every impulse to look backward. Already she was his, and she knew it.

He had taken her key and inserted it in the lock. The heavy door swung open easily.

CHAPTER SIX

'COME on, lazybones, get up!'

Marsh stood over Anna, his hands on his hips, the cheerful smirk on his lips plunged into shadow by the blinding light of the sun behind him.

'Mm-m, in a minute,' she purred. 'I like it here.'

The dry leaves crackling under her on the still-green grass were like a comfortable bed of straw. The cool of the earth under the warm blades of grass was so refreshing that she was loath to get up and continue walking.

'Come on, silly,' he prodded, dropping to his knee beside her. 'We're only up here for four days, so we have to keep moving. We've got exploring to do.'

'Uh-huh,' she smiled. 'Come here, you.' Grasping his shoulders, she pulled him down beside her and kissed his lips tenderly. 'That's adventurous enough for me,' she said.

'I see your point,' he agreed, returning her kiss with an intimacy that left her breathless. His hand strayed over her jacket, grazing the outline of her breasts under the suede, and came to rest beside her cheek. For a languorous moment he stroked her gently, contemplating the lush mane of her hair on its bed of leaves. The auburn waves seemed to take up the autumnal aura of their surroundings, as though Anna herself were a forest creature whose silken fur blended into the hues of the foliage around her.

She was gazing into his eyes with a calm he had not seen since he had known her. A slight smile of amusement on her lips, she toyed absently with the

99

fabric of his windbreaker, her eyes glowing with a strange, elfin satisfaction.

'Penny for your thoughts,' he said, his finger touching the soft skin beneath her ear.

'I love you,' she murmured.

Marsh smiled, a pained nostalgia coming over his features.

'When I think how long it took me to find you,' he said, 'and to hear you say those words. Five years in the same city, before you finally bumped into me!' With a theatrical shudder he banished the memory.

'I love you,' she repeated. 'You can hear it all you want, now. I love you, I love you, I love you.'

The exultation in her green eyes, framed by the hair splayed over the coloured leaves, was too bewitching to resist, and he bent to kiss her again. Her arms encircled him softly and, oblivious to the remote possibility that someone might pass, she hugged him to her, flexing her slender arms in an affectionate imitation of his own powerful embrace. With a histrionic gasp he made believe she had squeezed the wind out of him. But already his lips had touched the softness of her neck, and she felt his cool cheek against her own. Sandwiched between his warm body and the bed of leaves under her, she felt a mysterious peace enfold her, and lay motionless, her arms around him.

The sun glinted among fiery leaves as the branches of the huge oak swayed above her. Crisp autumnal odours were everywhere. Here at Crystal Lake, just as Marsh had predicted, the fall was considerably more advanced than in Chicago—and incomparably beautiful. Luck had been with them, and the Lake was warmed by fresh Indian summer air so pleasant that one nearly felt tempted to have a swim. The long walks they had taken through the many woods near the inn were like so many purifications, freeing Anna from the city's tensions and from her own painful memories.

Within minutes of her agreement to marry him, Marsh had been on the telephone, making hurried arrangements for a wedding in Judge Bardwell's chambers. Anna, feeling her excitement grow by leaps and bounds, had called Sally to explain the urgency of the situation. It was all happening so fast that her head was spinning as though in a pleasant dream.

Judge Bardwell had done his best to superimpose a stern, judicial expression over his approving smile.

'Mr Hamilton,' he said impishly, 'can you give this court one good reason why you deserve this beautiful woman?'

Sally had stood by, her eyes lit with the puckish satisfaction of the matchmaker, as the brief ceremony was performed. Several of Marsh's colleagues from the firm arrived, laden with bottles of champagne and makeshift wedding presents. The air seemed charged with humour and affection on all sides.

'I'm so happy for you, Anna,' Sally had smiled, kissing her sister. 'I know you've made the right decision.'

And in a whirl of activity which left Anna breathless, it was over. She found herself in the car with Marsh, embarked on the long drive to northern Wisconsin. A soft smile played over his lips as she held his hand. The highway flowed under them like a moving ribbon in the cool autumn air. And as afternoon turned to dusk, and the car's headlights illuminated the wooded expanse all around, Marsh and Anna talked and talked, filled with plans for the days ahead and the life together that awaited them. The fellings of release, of unaccustomed calm he had brought her over the past week blossomed now into a great glow of peace and happy expectation in the warm quiet of the car.

At last it seemed everything would be all right. Dazzled by the sudden transition her life had made from utter desperation to heady excitement, Anna clung to Marsh as the one clear beacon that showed the way to her future. During their late supper at the hotel, she found herself gazing into his eyes with an eager avidity that made her blush.

After tipping the sleepy bellboy. Marsh turned to her, his eyes filled with humour and tenderness.

'Well,' he said. 'Mrs Hamilton, is it?'

'Mrs Hamilton,' she smiled from the bed.

'At last,' he murmured, enfolding her in his powerful arms.

And the last traces of her unhappiness seemed banished for ever by the calm yielding she felt in his embrace. Finally she could accept him, open herself to him without second thoughts, experience the fiery intimacy of his lovemaking without an inner struggle to dominate the emotions that bound her to him. And it was a magical sense of sudden belonging that shuddered through her as she grasped and caressed him, certain at last that she was his for ever.

After what seemed a long dream of pure rapture, pleasure had given way to happy exhaustion in her, and she fell into a sweet, refreshing sleep in his arms.

Now, as she lay on the cool grass, her body warmed by the nearness of the man she loved, she felt a flutter in her senses which was instantly echoed by a subtle quickening in the touch of his flesh against her own.

'Let's go back,' Marsh murmured into her ear. 'We'll explore later.'

He felt her nod, and in a single lithe movement he had arisen, pulling her gently to her feet beside him. His hand rested quietly on her hip as they walked through the crackling leaves towards the inn. The sun shone through the boughs of the trees with a sharp, bracing brilliance, as though in celebration of a holiday from which all care and melancholy were banished. The crisp freshness of the world around them was a harmonious counterpoint to the hidden heat that linked them.

'Anna,' he said with sudden seriousness, 'we've talked a lot since we got up here, but you've never really told me how you came to leave N.T.E.L. I never asked Bob Samuels or anyone else about it, because I thought you'd want to tell me yourself sooner or later. Do you want to talk about it?'

Disturbed by the thoughts his question gave rise to in her own mind, she held herself closer to him.

'No,' she said. 'I just want to be with you.'

'You're sure?'

'It wasn't very important,' she said, 'and it's all over now. Now that I'm with you . . .'

'Okay,' he smiled, hugging her as they walked. 'As long as you feel you can put it behind you. But remember: we're married now, and you can tell me anything. If they treated you badly, you've got me to complain to, if you want.'

'I'm not in a complaining mood,' Anna laughed. 'I was happy there for a few years, and then not so happy. I don't blame N.T.E.L. itself. It was just a thing that didn't work out.'

She was disturbed to keep her chagrin over N.T.E.L. a secret, at the beginning of a new life, a new commitment to Marsh. But the episode, and the memory of Porter Deman, was too loathesome a thing to bring to mind now. She simply could not allow it to trouble the happiness to which she clung with all her heart.

Besides, she knew how upset and angry Marsh

would be if she told him of Porter Deman's vicious, clumsy attempts at seduction. The insult to her integrity would pain Marsh deeply, and she couldn't help fearing that he would make up his mind to punish Porter with some sort of retribution. Now was no time for revenge, and Marsh was a man capable of strong emotions.

But she could not forget Debby's opinion that something should be done to stop Porter Deman, for the sake of his future victims. When her honeymoon was over, she resolved, she would discuss the whole situation dispassionately with Marsh. His knowledge that Anna herself was no longer imperilled directly by it would insure his objectivity. She was more than confident that, with his intelligence and resourcefulness, he would know how to take action against so outrageous an injustice.

They would decide what to do together, she determined. But there was no point in spoiling the peaceful closeness of their honeymoon by pondering so distressing a topic. For now, she coveted all the happiness she could find with Marsh. She must derive strength from her love for him, and try to forget the last and most desperate moments of her life without him.

She stood silent by his side in the warm corridor as he turned the key in the heavy lock. With a muffled swish, the door swung back over the thick carpet and they were inside the room. The bright afternoon light shone gaily through the window, and then vanished in shadows as he pulled the curtains shut. The quiet beige walls, with their assortment of landscapes painted in dark hues, were plunged into darkness. Only a pale rim of light remained at the top of the curtains.

A curiosouly sensual feeling crept over Anna as she stood in the darkness, her eyes half shut, listening to the sounds made by Marsh's movements about the room. It was as though a deliberate silence had fallen between them, charged by their mutual knowledge of what was about to happen.

Her jacket lay on the chair now, and she had slipped off her shoes. She stood in her bare feet, consciously sensing the silky fabric of her blouse, the tightness of her jeans, on the alert flesh underneath. Her embrace with Marsh outside, in the cool air, had stirred her senses to a sudden tumult of desire, and she knew now that in a matter of seconds her impatient body would be naked again, free to spread its passion to the still air of the room, to melt with abandon into his own heat, to feel its excitement expand against his muscular limbs.

In this suspended moment, every fibre of her was tensed with pent-up wanting. Flares of ticklish passion throbbed under her clothes, clamouring for a release which would not be long in coming.

And that was the secret of the pleasure that taunted and excited her as she stood barefoot on the soft carpet. She felt as though there was a subtle nudity in the room itself, a mysterious nakedness to all the surfaces, the soft sounds, the quiet corners surrounding her. She could feel the taut, vibrant expanse of her own skin, breathing this charged air, and each current that touched the downy flesh of her arms, her legs, her cheek, was itself a knowing caress.

He was coming closer now. With a sort of wild attention she stood with her eyes closed, contemplating this last split second before he would touch her. An inner tremor told her she could not bear it longer.

As though he had read her thoughts, Marsh stood silent before her. His lips were the first part of him to touch her, and for a long moment they stood that way, an intimate, warm kiss their only contact. Although the very soul within her strained so urgently outward that she could barely keep from throwing herself at him with shameless abandon, Anna manged to remain somehow in that throbbing immobility.

Time seemed to hesitate, to wait upon itself and speed up with little jarring thrusts. Now, at last, the surface of his strong, unclothed body grazed her gently, and his hands slid over the fabrics that covered her. For a moment he caressed her hips, her arms, as though his touch were amused, titillated by the clothes that separated him from her. But already his fingertips had reached recesses, slender curves, that quickened so tempestuously under their passage that he knew he must free her now from her coverings.

With subtle expertise the gentle touch of his hands loosened her jeans, her blouse, passed languidly over her back and left her bra hanging undone on her shoulders. Bit by bit, curve by curve, her flesh opened itself to the air under his caress, her increasing nudity seeming a mobile, musical thing which drove them both to a tumult of silent wanting in the darkness.

As hard as she tried to concentrate on this teasing rhythm that stripped her slowly, the haze of desire in which she bathed was too bewitching to penetrate, and she came to herself already naked, her soft skin feeling the hardness of his body against her. The mystery of his man's flesh, so muscular, so incisive, and yet all softened into a sweet gentleness that moulded itself to her own soft curves, hyponotised her. And as waves of response flicked across her breasts, her thighs, her shoulders, at each contact with his warm, magnetic flesh, she felt herself go to him, press against him with a thousand little shudders. In its wild independence, her body moved with him and spoke to him in a language all its own.

As he bore her easily to the bed, placing her on the

soft comforter so gently that she felt almost weightless in his arms, it seemed there was no limit to the terrible intimacy with which he overwhelmed her senses. The profound inner tingle that quickened at the very sight of him, and erupted into waves of passion as his lips and hands drove her to ecstatic heights, was at the heart of her woman's body.

She knew she could keep no secret from the man behind the body that covered her now, in this dark room charged with pleasure. Underneath her visible personality, he knew how to make her talk, through her sighs, the responses of her limbs, in the language that he understood. Such was the penetrating power of her intimacy with him, this sensual delight that fed itself on her love for him. He was already rooted so deeply inside her that he must immediately sense every corner of doubt, of fear, of pain that might separate her from him.

And now, as a greater urgency came over their movements, melding them in an enormous, heated embrace, Anna forgot her cautious thoughts and gave herself to him utterly. Last night she had tasted the heady joy of making love to Marsh for the first time; today she knew the full meaning of belonging to him.

At last she lay quietly in his embrace, calmed and soothed by the weight of the hand resting on her breast, her little gasping breaths giving way to a slow, regular respiration as she rested her head on his shoulder. It was no wonder, she thought, that sensual intimacy was called a knowing of a person. Marsh knew her now, for he had stolen into her very heart, had felt her love fill up her whole personality in response to him. And she could trust him never to abuse the power that knowledge gave him.

Recalling his tactful questions about her misfortune at N.T.E.L., she looked forward to the day when she

would tell him the whole truth. It would be wonderful
to unburden herself with total trust in this sharply
introspective man. But all that mattered now was the
wonderful security of being with him, knowing that
she was no longer alone, that she would never be alone
again.

'Penny for your thoughts,' he whispered.

A great exultation suddenly took possession of her,
and she squirmed to her knees beside him, her lips
close to his own.

'I love you,' she smiled. 'Now give me my penny.'

His kiss was her reward.

In his own way, Marsh must have sensed the
mysterious message of utter trust and commitment
carried by the deep passion of their lovemaking, for in
the days that followed his demeanour reflected a quiet
joy in Anna's company. Few words were spoken
between them. Somehow the touch of their hands and
the glances they exchanged seemed to say all that was
required. The meaning of their relationship was clear
to both, and their every gesture was a promise to
depend on each other and to make whatever sacrifices
might become necessary to insure the success of their
marriage. Over and over again, they plighted their
troth through the affection in their words, their smiles,
and the utter closeness of their lovemaking.

The four days at Crystal Lake passed as though in a
sunlit dream. Like a steadfast partner in their
happiness, the Indian summer warmth persisted
throughout their stay. Everywhere they walked, trees
aflame with colour stood stately against the clear blue
sky, their leaves fluttering gently, as though conversing
with the breeze that caressed them. The lake's limpid
water was like a magic mirror reflecting not only the
rocks of its bottom, but also the brilliant hues of the

foliage on its shores. Everywhere their walks took them, a deep autumnal pungency greeted them, serving as a poetic backdrop to their own feelings. It was a change of season, a natural ferment of the woods' life which seemed to celebrate the change that had brought them together.

The long drive back to Chicago was not filled with excited conversation, as had been the trip to Crystal Lake. Instead, as the north woods gave way to rolling farmland, and finally to the flat vistas of Illinois, a silence made of pure fulfilment and understanding lay between them, punctuated now and then by a happy remark, a laugh, a caress.

Marsh's apartment, located in a skyscraper that towered above the Loop, was all that Anna might have expected. Its tasteful décor, highlighted by functional modern furniture, glass surfaces, and clear white walls, reflected his solid masculinity and his impatience with frills of any kind. He threw open the curtains to reveal a dazzling vista which included the river, the Marina Towers, the Wrigley Building.

'Marsh, it's wonderful!' Anna exclaimed.

'Think you can stand it here?'

'I'd go anywhere with you,' she smiled.

With a look of amused concentration, he showed her all the rooms, pausing at the large closet in the bedroom.

'Think you can get all your clothes in there?' he asked with a critical frown.

'Certainly,' she said. 'I don't have that many. My salary has never allowed a lot of buying.'

'That will change now,' he smiled. 'I want you to have a wardrobe that suits your every mood. As long,' he added, hugging her, 'as you don't mind taking those clothes off once in a while.'

It was agreed that Anna would take a cab to her

apartment tomorrow to pick up her clothes and a few
personal effects. Marsh would have a full day of work,
but promised to be home early. In the days to come
Anna would see to clearing out her apartment and
finding room for everything in her new home. After a
good long rest, she would decide whether to look for
work.

'The honeymoon isn't over yet,' smiled Marsh.
'We're going to enjoy ourselves. And there's no time,'
he added, trapping her suddenly in his powerful arms,
'like the present.'

'Well, how's the newlywed?' asked Marsh's secretary
as he entered the office the next morning.

'Never better, Mary. Did you all manage to survive
without me?'

'In a manner of speaking,' she sighed.

'Where's John?'

'He's with Harold and a couple of lawyers. They
want you to meet them for lunch. It's about a murder.'

'Murder?' Marsh feigned surprise. 'In this town? I
don't believe it.'

'Your mail is waiting,' she added as he pushed open
the door of his office.

After opening the window to let in some fresh air,
Marsh stood over his desk, sorting through envelopes
and manila folders and doing his best to recall the state
of his case load before he left for Wisconsin. There
was work to be done, and he would have to have a talk
with his partners about pending cases.

'What's this?' he wondered absently, opening a
letter bearing the N.T.E.L. logo. 'Oh, yes,' he smiled.
In his concern about Anna's difficulties in finding a
job, he had had Mary write N.T.E.L. for her
personnel file, on the pretext that she was applying for
work with his firm. In the excitement of his marriage

and honeymoon he had forgotten all about the request. Now he recalled his curiosity as to whether the company had somehow mistreated Anna, and he felt the furtive thrill of the eavesdropper as he prepared to see what her bosses thought of her.

His face became serious as he tossed the secretary's covering letter aside and began to read the computer's file. After a moment he sat down at his desk, reading and then re-reading the words before him.

'I don't believe it,' he murmured, glancing about the room before perusing the file for a third time. Finally he put the letter down and stood up to pace the office.

It was simply too much to take in all at once. Anna, a thief ? A security risk . . . And the other part, the part about offering herself sexually in exchange for leniency. It couldn't be! That couldn't be Anna Halpern, Anna Hamilton they were talking about. It was unbelievable.

God knows, he thought, she did seem terribly upset last week and the week before. It was obvious there was some kind of trouble. And no wonder she wasn't getting anywhere in the job market, with this thing in her personnel file. But an accusation of such enormity! What in hell had she done to deserve this? There must be some sort of mistake. They must have mixed her up with somebody else.

Quickly he turned back to the desk and read the damning document once more. No, there was no mistake. It was Anna, all right. They had all her numbers, her job record.

Marsh stared out the window in perplexity. 'Well,' he thought, 'I can understand why she didn't want to talk about this.' In retrospect, it was clear she must have had some inkling of what was going on. Otherwise, why the air of desperation, of depression, of pained reticence about her termination? But why hadn't she told him about it? What was she hiding? If she was innocent, there must be some explanation for this unbelievable smear. If she was innocent . . .

Remembering his lawyer's instincts, he tried to imagine the circumstances that could have led to such a thing. But nothing made sense. If it were all some kind of crazy frame-up, then why hadn't they prosecuted her? So much malice breathed through the lines of that text that it seemed inconceivable they wouldn't have had her arrested. Unless they had their doubts . . .

But the accusation was so unequivocal, so over-whelming. Who would make up a thing like that? Suppose she was guilty, even if the idea strained credulity. Why would she do it? Fear? Blackmail? What about the people who put her up to it? Perhaps they weren't satisfied, when she failed. Perhaps that was who was on the phone that night, when Anna suddenly became so upset.

What had she said? '*That's out of the question.*' And then: '*Where?*' Such secretive talk. She couldn't have been so upset about the simple difficulty of finding another job. She had to know what was going on.

So she was desperate, for whatever reason. She had nowhere to turn. Knew she wouldn't find another job, knew that that thing was in her file. Or feared that it was. And she had her sister to worry about . . .

'So what did she do?' he thought, sitting down heavily to blunt the realisation. 'She married me.

'That's why she agreed so abruptly. It was the day after that enigmatic phone call. I didn't seriously expect her to agree without a lot of thought, a long delay. I concluded it was love that was motivating her. Perhaps it was desperation.'

He struggled confusedly to adjust his own mental

image of Anna to the picture painted by the personnel file. Anna was the essence of honesty, self-respect, pride. The file described someone who undertook illegal behaviour for the benefit of an unidentified conspirator. For money? Or political reasons? Or both ... And the offer of sexual favours seemed to indicate either an utterly loathesome personality or, perhaps, some sort of blind commitment to a cause. But none of this made sense when ascribed to Anna.

With a sinking feeling he suddenly imagined her using him, marrying him through some ulterior motive. It was too fantastic to believe, but it hurt.

'Well, I'll just have to get it out of her,' he thought. It had been one thing to respect her privacy when all he knew was that she was having trouble finding a job. It was quite another to keep silent about so outrageous a discovery.

She would probably have an explanation. There was no sense in getting angry until he had heard her out. But in spite of his resolution to be reasonable, he felt a dark anger in his heart. Whatever the explanation, she had presumed to marry him without ever having confided in him about so grave a matter. She had simply assumed that he was not worthy of her trust.

But surely, if she was innocent, she would have spoken up! As he stood alone in his office, Marsh found it more and more difficult to believe Anna could be blameless, even though the deeds ascribed to her seemed out of character. She must have done something, something blameworthy, to get herself into this mess.

Her image was receding from his mind's eye, becoming less and less familiar, more alien and disconcerting, as he thought over the revelations in the file. He found himself wondering in consternation at his own haste in marrying this woman he knew so little. Perhaps she was motivated by things she had kept from him. Who knew? Perhaps there were parts of her life, her character, that he knew nothing about.

'*I want you and need you*,' he had insisted in his innocence as he proposed to her. '*I don't need to know any more.*' How hollow those words rang now!

He recalled his unspoken speculations about the men in Anna's life. She was a strikingly beautiful woman, clearly not the type to lead a life without involvements with the opposite sex. There must be a man in this plot somewhere. A contact, a boss—something.

Now he remembered his visceral impression that the person on the phone that night, whose words had elicited such terse replies from Anna, was a man. '*Where?*' she had asked, turning her back to Marsh as she spoke into the phone.

The torments of jealousy began to add themselves to his already painful thoughts. He imagined Anna engaged in behaviour he had never dreamed possible. He imagined her attempt to seduce the boss who had confronted her with the evidence against her. The idea of her offer, her proposition, the expression she must have had on her face, as seductive as possible ... It was intolerable.

'No,' he said aloud, shaking off his suspicions. 'She'll have an explanation. There's no sense in jumping to conclusions. But, by God, she'll tell me what the hell is going on, or I'll ...'

Suddenly the most disturbing thought of all struck him. There was Sally. Suppose, for the sake of argument, that Anna did what she did for money. God knew she needed it for Sally's education, since their parents' deaths had left them without a nickel. Suppose she failed to accomplish her mission and was not paid by whoever put her up to it. Then, having lost her job, she would have been desperate. She would not have known where to turn for money.

He recalled his own cajoling efforts to persuade her to marry him. *'We'll help Sally finish college,'* he had said. *'Money will be no problem.'* Obviously Anna had taken him at his word.

And only last night he had insisted on taking care of Sally's pending tuition payments immediately, so that his new wife's lingering financial worries could be dissipated without further ado. He had laughed off Anna's protesting complaints about her own insolvency, belittling the very idea of money and its attendant woes.

'If you want to pay me back,' he had grinned, 'just step right over here.' The delightful, soft kiss she had placed on his lips had seemed an almost disproportionate payment for so insubstantial an amount.

But it could not have seem insubstantial to her, in her desperate need.

'What a sucker I've been,' he thought. 'No Surprises Hamilton! Well, I've had the surprise of my life this time.' As a successful lawyer who was more than vulnerable to Anna's charms, he had appeared on the scene just in time to serve as her escape from the predicament she found herself in. How fortunate for her that he was walking down that N.T.E.L. corridor at the propitious moment! And within two weeks she had become his wife . . .

The two images of Anna began to cease contradicting each other. Now he could picture an Anna who stooped to illegal and perhaps despicable actions out of desperate loyalty to her sister. Including marrying a man she had just met—a man who was obviously hellbent on marrying her as soon as possible.

'Come on,' he upbriaded himself, 'take it easy. Get

control of yourself. There's an answer to all this, and you'll find it.'

But the tormenting thoughts that assailed him would not cease their cacophony inside his mind. Angry with himself, with Anna, and with this whole mess which had suddenly thrown his life into chaos, he slammed the desk drawer on the file and left the office.

CHAPTER SEVEN

ANNA heard the unfamiliar sound of Marsh's key in the lock just as she had finished her preparations for dinner. It had been a busy, happy day. After a restful sleep, she had had coffee with Marsh this morning and then journeyed to her old apartment. Its bland, forlorn furnishings, which for so long had been the scene of her loneliness, had the look of relics. The patina of time seemed already to have marked them with a prehistoric aura. They were the personal effects of someone who no longer existed: Anna Halpern, solitary working woman. Now she could move among them with easy confidence, picking out an item here and there to take across the city to her new home, her new life. The rest would soon fade into oblivion as the old flat was rented to a stranger.

It was a heady feeling, tinged with the childish excitement of a holiday. Even the rays of sunshine streaming in the window had lost their faded look, and seemed to radiate from that high place across the city where life had begun anew for her. After gathering her clothes in suitcases and filling a box with the things she needed most, she had helped the friendly cab driver carry it all downstairs. How strange it felt to ride a cab through the Loop! The city seemed so elegant, so vibrantly metropolitan, that Anna could not help experiencing a tourist's excitement as theatres, department stores, famous Chicago landmarks passed by.

After putting her things away in the large bedroom closet and bureau, she studied Marsh's kitchen.

Although the refrigerator was nearly empty, the cupboards and spice rack confirmed the impression made by the meal he had cooked at her flat. He was indeed a good cook, and had had occasion to buy most of the ingredients needed for gourmet recipes. Sitting with a cup of coffee before the magnificent picture window, Anna made a short list of groceries to buy. She wanted to make him something special tonight, to welcome him home to his first evening of married life.

For a few precious moments she sat gazing at the urban vista outside the window, allowing herself to savour the novelty of the situation. She was actually to live here, in this apartment, with the handsome man who had swept her off her feet from the first instant she had seen him. It all seemed too good to be true.

At last, afraid her bubble would burst if she dwelt too long on her happiness, she had gone out to an unfamiliar downtown grocery store and bought what she needed. And now the preparations were finished.

'Welcome home,' she smiled, rising to greet him.

His kiss was less than passionate as he rested his hand on her shoulder before throwing his briefcase on a chair.

'Hard day?' she asked, imagining the busy schedule he had left in abeyance during their honeymoon.

'In more ways than one,' he grunted.

'Would you like a drink?' she asked, feeling her happy mood dissolve under a nameless trepidation.

'I'll make it.' He disappeared into the kitchen. She heard the sound of ice being dropped into his glass.

'I'm making you something special tonight,' she called. There was no answer. Instead, she heard cupboards being opened and closed, the muffled thump of the refrigerator door. After a moment he crossed to the bedroom, drink in hand, without saying a word.

After two minutes that seemed an eternity to Anna, he emerged dressed in slacks and a sweater, and sat down with a sigh in the chair facing her. His expression was pained, distracted.

'You look tired,' she said tentatively. 'Had a lot of work piled up while we were gone?'

Marsh grunted. 'You never know,' he said darkly, 'what's going to pop up when you turn your back for a second.'

'Is it still the hard case you mentioned last week?' she asked.

'They're all hard,' he said without looking at her, his jaw set in a rigid, unhappy look. 'The hardest part,' he went on, darting her a significant glance, 'is trying to get people to tell you the truth. Everyone is always hiding something.'

Silence fell again as he finished his drink and strode to the kitchen to get another. It was clear something was wrong. Anna had never seen Marsh's accustomed cheerfulness disappear in so total a manner, and she was forced to reflect that she had not known him long enough to be familiar with all his moods. On the other hand, his demeanour seemed far too enigmatic and even dangerous to be explained by a mere mood. Something must be seriously wrong.

He returned to his chair, giving her an inscrutable glance as he sat down.

'Is something the matter, Marsh?' she asked, unable to bear this stony silence a minute longer. 'You don't seem to be yourself.'

'A lot of people,' he retorted with ill-concealed anger, 'are not quite themselves, I discover. Not quite what they seem.'

'What do you mean?'

'You think you know someone,' he said. 'You think you understand a situation. Then you find out you've been ignorant of the real facts of the case, because someone has been misrepresenting himself, in order to try to hoodwink you. It isn't fun being a dupe, Anna, believe me.'

'I don't understand,' she said. 'What case are you talking about?'

'It's a little closer to home than that, my love,' he said darkly.

'Why don't you tell me what you're getting at?' she asked, flushing under his accusing stare. 'Must you talk in circles?'

'I've been going around in circles for quite some time,' he said, arising suddenly and seizing his briefcase. 'If it hadn't been for one little break, one little accident, I might have gone on that way for ever.'

'Marsh,' she pleaded, genuinely frightened by his words and his scowling aspect, 'what are you talking about?'

'There,' he said, throwing the letter on the coffee table before her. 'Read it for yourself, Anna. Then explain it to me, if you can.'

Fearfully she opened the envelope, although the sight of the N.T.E.L. logo and address already sufficed to tell her that something grave had happened.

At first the impersonal message, headed by her name, Social Security number, and address, seemed merely strange—a curious eavesdropping on her identity, intended to be passed among others. Then the horrifying words of the file began to sink in.

A great chill went through her limbs as she saw the monstrous extent of Porter Deman's chicanery. It had been one thing to realise that she was not finding a new job because Porter had done something, some obscure thing to harm her. It was quite another to see her name vilified, her character assassinated, in the text of this official document. It was as though the whole company, the gigantic N.T.E.L. corporation, had acquiesced in this malignant plan to spread evil lies about her to any employer who would listen.

'My God,' she thought, feeling faint from the shock of seeing the file. 'My God!' But she said nothing. Over and over again, she read the words in stunned disbelief. Distantly, she heard the sound of the ice clinking in Marsh's glass. He had gone back to the kitchen, probably to make himself another drink.

'No wonder,' she thought. 'After what he must think of me now.'

Her emotions seemed to have retreated to a faraway corner of her mind, and warred chaotically with each other. She felt so cold that she thought she must be pale as a ghost. In her numbness she did not notice the tears which ran silently down her cheeks.

She heard his voice as though across a gulf of shadow.

'See what I mean?' he said cruelly, triumphantly. 'You never know what you're going to find out about someone you thought you knew pretty well.'

'Where did you get this?' she heard herself ask.

'What difference does it make where I got it?' he shot back.

'No, I meant ... I mean ...' Her words came out chaotically, uncontrollably. She had to struggle to determine what she wanted to say.

'It isn't true,' she said at last. 'It isn't true.'

He sat in silence across the room.

'Then what is true?' he asked at length. 'Just what the hell *is* true about you, Anna? You've been lying to me for so long, hiding things from me for so long, I think it's about time you said one true thing to me.'

'I haven't lied to you,' she protested lamely.

'That's a good one,' he laughed bitterly. 'The first

time I ever met you, you claimed you were quite
ignorant of your company's inner workings. A small
cog, you called yourself. Apparently you understated
your expertise.'

'That was true,' she said, acutely aware that the
document before her contradicted her words.

'But that was only the beginning,' he shrugged off
her denial. 'You saw fit to tell me that you left
N.T.E.L. because things "weren't working out", as
you put it. At the time, I saw no reason to suspect
there was anything more to it. I let myself believe that
you and the company had simply become incompatible,
for some reason of convenience or personality, or
whatever. Are you going to tell me that was true as
well?'

Anna shook her head. 'No,' she admitted, 'that was
not true.'

'Well,' Marsh smiled ironically, 'at least we've made
a step in the right direction. Where shall we go from
here? Let's see . . . I've seen your sister, so I know she
really exists. There's no point in wondering whether
you made her up along with your other lies. And the
cheque I put in the mail for her tuition this morning
was real enough. As soon as the university cashes it,
I'll be able to set my mind at rest on that score. How
about your parents? Are they really dead? Are you
really from Bloomington?'

'Don't be cruel, Marsh. Please!' The tears inundat-
ing her flushed cheeks belied her expression of
stunned panic. 'I've never lied to you. I just couldn't
. . . talk about what happened.'

'You'll talk about it now,' he warned. 'And you'd
better talk straight, Anna.'

Shocked into momentary silence by the enormity of
the situation, Anna tried desperately to think. But the
obscene success of Porter Deman's evil design seemed

overwhelming. After having cost her her job and preventing her from finding another one, he had managed to come between her and the husband she loved. It seemed every bit as futile to explain herself to Marsh as to convince a prospective employer that the file was full of lies. The letter was official. It carried the weight of the company itself, and emerged from the endless banks of computers which made up not only N.T.E.L., but the whole business establishment of the city, the nation. How could she bluntly deny what was there in black and white, for all to see?

'I'm waiting,' said Marsh, a sardonic smile curling his lips.

'All right,' she began miserably, 'I'll try to explain.' Every corner of her body, only recently cleansed and purified by her intimacy with Marsh, suddenly curled up on itself, stung by the nausea of her memory of Porter Deman. The evil she had seen incarnated in the file seemed to penetrate her like a poison, making her feel unclean and violated, as though in this very moment Porter Deman's vile hands still reached out towards her. And in truth, had he not found a way to invade the very privacy of her marriage, to transform her loving husband into the hurt, accusing figure who now stared at her without trust?

'None of it is true,' she insisted. 'I can't understand how he ... how this happened. They know, at N.T.E.L., that this isn't true.'

'They know,' he mimicked pitilessly, 'that what they themselves have attested to in your personnel file is a lie? You must be kidding, Anna.'

'I mean,' she persisted, 'they assured me there would be nothing in the file, even though they had to ... fire me.' Her hand rose to her knitted brow as she tried to sort out the confusing facts thronging her mind.

'But that's exactly what the file says,' Marsh taunted her. 'That you tried to convince them not to make any of it official. You have a lot of explaining to do, Anna.'

'Please,' she sighed, 'let me finish.' But she could hardly find words to describe the miasma of misfortune created by Porter Deman. Though she knew the truth was her only ally, her shame and disbelief paralysed her. How could she explain away so complex and convincing a web of lies?

'I'll tell you,' she said, turning pale, 'what I told the Vice-President when this whole thing began. I never saw the file they claim was in my desk. I never pulled it from the computer. It was . . . it was all the work of one man. He did this to me. As for the part about attempting to . . . to seduce . . .' Her eyes filled with tears once more, and she could not suppress a sob of pain and exasperation. 'That is a lie—a horrid, awful lie.'

'What man?' asked Marsh. 'What are you talking about? Your own Vice-President's signature is under this text. Are you trying to tell me he's framing you?'

'No.' She shook her head, trying to clear the cobwebs caused by this complicated dilemma about which Marsh knew nothing. 'Another man. Someone from N.T.E.L. He tried to force me to . . . do something improper. When I wouldn't, he told me I'd be fired. The next day I was fired—because of this classified file business. I knew he was behind it, but there was nothing I could do. Mr Robbins didn't believe me, but he said he wouldn't mention the incident in my personnel file, so that I would be able to find another job in the field. Then I couldn't find a job, and . . . and this is obviously why. He did this— the other man. He even told me . . .'

'What man?' asked Marsh. 'What was improper? What do you mean when you say he told you? How could Robbins not know about this, since it's over his own signature? You're not making sense, Anna. You'd better start telling a more coherent story. Or is it too hard to make up a thing like this on the spur of the moment? Is that it?'

A curious sensation stole insidiously through Anna. How loathsome it was to be a victim, a prey. The passivity of the role seemed to penetrate to one's very bones. Trapped, immobilised by the staring eyes which demanded that she submit, that she do the will of someone else, or suffer the consequences ... A profound, resentful anger began to alloy her terrified sense of guilt. How long was this bondage to continue? How long must she continue to cower under the imperious stares of severe, demanding men?

'I'm waiting, Anna.'

For a cruel instant Marsh's deep voice brought back the memory of Porter Deman speaking the same words as he sat rocking in his desk chair under the painting on his office wall. '*I'm waiting, Anna . . .*'

She looked up at Marsh. Even the power of her love was not sufficient to dissipate the sudden suspicion she felt. Just like Porter Deman, like Charles Robbins, like all the polite but demanding personnel managers she had had interviews with, Marsh was immured within his prideful man's preoccupations. He sat there, in his wounded masculinity, turning all his energies to his accusation of her. His pride was hurt by the revelation that he did not possess every shred of information about her private life. He was making no effort to listen or understand, but only to accuse.

'I didn't tell you about this,' she said firmly, 'because it was too horrible, and upsetting, and . . .' she searched for the word which would describe her state of mind, 'unjust. Perhaps I was wrong, but I wanted to leave it behind me. The charges are false.

They were concocted by an executive who had a personal grudge against me. I know for a fact that he is responsible for this file, as he was for the original accusation.'

'Who?' Marsh asked, his black eyes glittering with a light so dangerous that Anna felt a shudder of real fear before him. 'Who did this? What personal grudge? What improper thing?'

Anna shook her head, tormented by his stabbing questions. A great surge of impotent anger possessed her. She could not bear to be humiliated further by the web of lies surrounding her. And even though she knew her resentment against Marsh was not entirely justified, she felt that her agony of useless self-defence must stop somewhere.

'He wanted me to go to bed with him,' she said at last, feeling darkly indifferent to the consequences of her revelation. 'I wouldn't do it, so he took his revenge.'

'Who?' The menacing intensity in Marsh's voice was almost unbearable to hear.

'I told Charles Robbins the man's name,' said Anna, feeling suddenly, pridefully alone. 'I suggested that he investigate the situation for himself. But I see no reason to tell you his name, Marsh. To be frank, it's none of your business. He's the company's problem now. If they let him get away with an ugly thing like this,' she glanced at the tear-stained document, 'so be it. I'm finished with them.'

'But you're not finished with me,' said Marsh. 'Not yet, anyway. If you expect me to believe this story—which seems, by the way, a little less credible with every detail you add—you'd better make a clean breast of it. And I'd suggest you start with the name of the man you say is your accuser.'

His taut limbs seemed coiled in a lethal readiness for

action as he sat before her. Anna dared not speculate
on what he might do if she gave him the information
he wanted. Again she had to remind herself that she
did not know Marsh well enough to predict what
extremities his anger could force him to.

Besides, she reflected, the important thing was his
relationship with her. The punishment of Porter
Deman was the affair of N.T.E.L.

'No,' she shook her head determinedly. 'I've told
you the truth. You don't need his name. It's not your
place to get involved in this, Marsh. I don't know how
you came by this file, but . . .'

'I had my secretary write to N.T.E.L. for it,' he
interrupted. 'Before our marriage. I knew you were
having some sort of trouble, and since you weren't
forthcoming about it, I decided to find out for myself.'

'I see,' she shot back angrily. 'As though it wasn't
bad enough to know that there were slanderous
documents circulating about me behind my back, now
I find that my own husband has been spying on me, as
well! You had no right, Marsh.'

'Normal rules were suspended,' he shrugged
ironically, 'since the woman I was about to marry
lacked the confidence in me to reveal that she was
in bad trouble. I thought I might be able to help
you.'

'No one could help me,' Anna insisted. 'He'd
planned it so that I would be accused of breaching
security before I had a chance to complain about his
behaviour towards me. There was no way for me to
convince my superiors I was telling the truth.'

'There would have been,' he corrected, 'if you had
been telling the truth. You could have taken legal
action to force them to prove their accusation against
you. And when this personnel file came out, which
you now claim you were aware of, you could have

produced it as clear evidence of malice. That alone would have convinced a judge that you were the victim of a deliberate plot, and had been deprived of your job illegally. They would have been forced to take you back, regardless of what they believed—assuming they were prejudiced. But you did none of these things, and two things resulted.'

'What things?' Chagrined to hear his lucid legal reasoning, Anna began to doubt the correctness of her actions.

'In the first place,' he said, 'you lost your job and your career, since this file made you unemployable. And in the second place,' he said darkly, 'you married me.'

'I don't understand,' began Anna, stung by his conclusions. 'What are you saying?'

'It's simple, my love,' he answered. 'You were lying before, and you're lying now. What I'm saying is that I do not believe you.'

'Marsh!' she cried. 'You can't be serious! I've told you the truth. I was guilty of nothing!'

'But you never behaved like a person who was innocent,' he pursued. 'You behaved like a person who had been caught engaging in illegal conduct, and who moved on to greener pastures.'

'What's that supposed to mean?' As though she had been enveloped by a nightmare that refused to end, Anna saw the shade of Charles Robbins' calm incredulity in her own husband's eyes. *He doesn't believe me*, she thought desperately.

'It means,' he said, 'that you were out of a job, still responsible for your sister's education, and unable to find work. As luck would have it, your considerable charms managed to attract a suitor who had enough means to take care of your financial burdens. A gullible sort of fellow who wanted nothing more than to marry you, support you, and share your troubles. In the circumstances, you saw the line of least resistance, and you followed it.'

'I can't believe what I'm hearing,' muttered Anna, her heart sinking. 'You think I used you? That I married you for the sake of convenience?'

'The shoe certainly fits,' he shrugged. 'Your far-fetched story about a mystery man who manipulates the personnel department of a corporation in order to satisfy his personal grudges puts a bit of a strain on the imagination. If it were true, you would have sought legal advice. And,' he laughed bitterly, 'I was right there at the time. I'm a lawyer myself.'

'But I barely knew you,' Anna protested. 'I couldn't see involving you in my personal difficulties.'

'You knew me well enough to marry me, though, didn't you?' Angry triumph resounded in his deep voice as his logic coiled pitilessly around her. 'You married the man you wouldn't trust to help you. If that isn't using a person, I don't know what is.'

'You're twisting it all out of shape,' Anna objected in confusion. 'I may have been wrong, and as you say, I probably should have found legal help. But it seemed impossible to prove my innocence. When Mr Robbins fired me despite my work record at N.T.E.L., I felt I had no chance. I thought the battle was lost, and I wanted to put it behind me.'

'By marrying me.'

'No!' she cried, forcing herself to meet the black eyes which seemed to grip her cruelly. 'I did everything I could to find a job. Then I found out I wasn't going to succeed and . . .'

'And then you married me.'

'No, Marsh, you have it all wrong. I was desperate, and I was so ashamed . . . so disgusted by the whole thing. I just couldn't talk about it. But I married you for the simple reason that I loved you. You must believe that.'

'Why should I?' he asked. 'Since you didn't trust me enough to tell me the truth about yourself then, why should I believe you're being honest now?'

'Because I am!' Anna insisted. 'What I've said is true, Marsh—every word of it.'

'What do you suppose would happen,' he changed the subject, 'if I showed this file to Charles Robbins?'

'He'd be surprised,' said Anna, 'since it's been altered. That is, assuming he was telling me the truth when he promised to keep the original accusation out of it. But he would still believe I was guilty of the security breach, and that I deserved to be fired.'

'You're wrong,' Marsh corrected. 'If I showed him this, he'd see the malice immediately, and you'd have your job back in five minutes.'

'I wouldn't want it,' Anna said bitterly. 'The conditions at N.T.E.L. would still be the same. As a matter of fact, I suspect that Charles Robbins believed me in the first place. He knew I was a trustworthy employee. But it didn't matter. It was just as the other man said: regardless of whether I was believed, I would lose my job.'

'First you say Robbins didn't believe you, and then you say he did believe you.' Alert intelligence was combined with obvious distrust in Marsh's sharp eyes.

'Because it doesn't matter one way or the other,' Anna sighed. 'He told me it's company policy to fire anyone who is even accused of being a security risk. Besides,' she added, 'the person who . . . did this to me is in a position of responsibility. He's more important to the company than I ever was. My word could carry no weight against his, regardless of where the truth lay. That's why they can keep their job, as far as I'm concerned.'

'Your sour grapes aren't very convincing,' said Marsh. 'You claim you don't care that an injustice has been done you, and that your chosen career has been destroyed. You just want to leave it all behind you, as you say. In favour of what, Anna? Of marriage to a man you refused to invest a little trust in, but who happens to be well enough fixed to take care of your sister? Is that it?'

'Now you sound like a prosecutor,' Anna reproached him. 'I'm your wife, not a felon.'

'Not according to that,' he said, pointing to the file.

'So you don't believe me.' Anger welled up in Anna's frayed nerves, banishing her fears.

'There's no reason to,' he replied evenly. 'You have no credibility. You married me under false pretences; you made no attempt to defend yourself legally against what you claim was an injustice; at every turn you've covered up the truth instead of revealing it. That, Anna, is what a lawyer would say. From a husband's point of view it's much simpler. You have refused me your trust, so I see no reason to extend you my own.'

A bitter laugh escaped Anna's lips as she contemplated the enormity of her predicament.

'This is amazing,' she said. 'I've committed the unpardonable crime of being a victim. I've lost my job and my career. And now my own husband, after going behind my back to investigate my misfortunes, doesn't believe that I'm innocent. Have it your own way, then, Marsh. I've had enough.'

He had stood up.

'So have I,' he said. 'I don't think you deserve it, but I'll give you one last chance to tell me the name of this shadowy character you say is behind all this.'

'Why should I expect you to believe that?' asked Anna, infuriated by his imperious behaviour.

'You have a point there,' he agreed bitterly.

'Marsh,' she said suddenly as the terrible import of their quarrel came home to her, 'I love you. I couldn't tell you about this whole mess—it was too horrible. It was all happening just as I met you, and I wanted to put it behind me. But you must believe me. I intended to tell you everything once some time had gone by . . .'

'You mean once you were safely married and your bills were paid,' he interrupted.

Agonised by his cruel words, she made a last effort to convince him he was wrong. 'I wasn't keeping silent to protect myself,' she said.

'Then why?' he asked. 'To protect me? I hardly think so, Anna. I'm sorry, for you—for both of us.'

Marsh had thrown open the closet and seized a jacket. He opened the door to the corridor and stood in silence. An invisible force, powered by all the hopes accompanying her newfound love for him, struggled to turn her to him, to make her plead with him to come back. But something else, born of his obvious lack of trust and her own hurt, made her hesitate and turn in upon herself. And in that split second he must have sensed the inner conflict that kept her from him, for he closed the door abruptly and was gone.

Hours later Anna lay silently in his bed, having long ago given up her tossing and turning, for she was sure that sleep would not come this night.

After throwing away her uneaten dinner and doing the dishes, she had contemplated the apartment. The traces of her arrival were still sparse enough that she could erase them all by leaving now, tonight. It was simply a matter of packing her bags, re-packing the large box with books and personal effects, and calling a cab. She would sleep tonight in her own bed, miles away, and when he returned he would know she had accepted his assessment of their marriage. If he wanted his freedom back, let him have it.

On the other hand, he might return at any moment. It would be embarrassing to be caught in the process of packing her things. He might be angry. He might try to stop her.

Besides, what if his anger drove him to do something foolish? What if he drank too much, or got into some kind of trouble? She should be here in case he needed her.

But most of all, she could not bring herself to abandon him, even though it was he who had walked out on her. She prayed he would return, that he would not despair of their relationship so quickly. If he had a change of heart, she wanted to be here, so he would know she had waited. She herself could not give up so soon on this marriage that had seemed so wonderful only twenty-four hours ago. Perhaps Marsh would remember the happiness they had known these past days. Perhaps he would reconsider. In spite of her impulse to seize what remained of her independence, to go home alone, she could not deny that she needed him.

Sleep, held back by the state of her nerves, but abetted by her emotional exhaustion, crept stealthily over her, and her pained thoughts became tinged with dream fantasies. The blue surface of Crystal Lake hovered before her mind's eye, reflecting multitudes of bright autumn leaves, and rippled by the crisp breeze of Indian summer. She was back in the hotel room. Marsh was smiling again, touching her gently, intimately, as he had the night of their arrival. In his tall, taut presence, so vital and strong in his windbreaker, his jeans, he was so handsome. And he smiled. He was not angry . . .

She did not hear the quiet click of the outer door, or

the muted sounds of him taking off his clothes. The settling of his weight on the bed brought an unconscious purr of satisfaction from her, as she sensed his approach from within her dream. Even the quiet touch of his hand to her cheek, her hair, did not wake her, but stole through the confused levels of her consciousness to her senses, which reacted immediately to him.

For a long, sweet moment, her sleeping mind joined her aroused body in believing that the clock had truly been turned back. The hushed rustle of leaves persisted dreamily in the background of her growing desire. The darkness was that of the hotel room, plunged into daytime obscurity by his sudden closing of the curtains. The daunting warmth of his flesh closing over her own was again the penetrating intimacy it had been in the middle of that rapt afternoon.

Over and over again, in the confusion of her dream, Marsh's hands loosened her jeans, her shirt, her bra. Again and again the fabrics came loose, hung in a disarray produced by passion, slipped softly to the floor. Once more his hand crept to her breast and closed over the poised nipple which clamoured for his touch. Again she was naked, naked as though for the first time, her skin flicked tempestuously by the still, warm air of the silent room. And the hardness of his body grazed her soft curves, so magnetic, so powerful even in the most ethereal pressure. Her own sleek flesh, moving instinctively in its strange, rhythmic way, rubbed and touched him, kissed and released him, slipped luxuriantly over him, making of this contact a weird, teasing magic as old and irresistible as life itself.

Again and again, in this sensual dream fuelled silently by a reality of which she was not yet aware, his lips and hands drove her to a frenzy of wanting as the comforter slid beneath her. She was gripping him, running her slender fingers through his hair, returning his kisses with an abandon that stunned her senses. Closer he came, his touch penetrating ever deeper into the heady obscurity of her mind and soul, and she accepted him happily. The tickling, the teasing which had taunted her senses into an agony of desire were already expanding into that enormous fire of fulfilment, of ecstasy, in which he knew her utterly.

Slowly, in little dreamlike fits and starts, she came to herself in his bed. But in this awakening she was coming to him, losing herself in him, and finding herself once again through the passion he inspired in her. Aware now of the terror that had gripped her tonight, she clung to him desperately as his desire grew stronger. All at once the novelty of her surroundings struck her, adding its lush unfamiliarity to the wild probing of his touch. Before she could quite fathom what was happening, her passion was growing, preparing to spend itself here in the darkness with him. With a strength born of desire and fearful love, she grasped him, held him to her breast, as though to convince him that whatever had come between them, this intimacy still remained to bind them together, to provide some small hope that the damage might be undone, the clock turned back, the future saved.

The paroxysm had ended. Quietly Marsh receded from her embrace, and she felt sleep close over her like a soft coverlet. He was still beside her, warm and close, breathing deeply. Aware that he had come back to her despite the gulf between them, she clung to the hope promised by his physical presence, and slipped into an exhausted sleep by his side.

When she awoke, he was gone. After a day of restless activity in the apartment, she heard his key turn in the lock once more. His anger seemed gone now. In its place was a strange, disturbing aloofness. Unfailingly courteous and even attentive in his behaviour towards her, Marsh remained politely distant as he answered her questions, spoke in casual phrases of his work, and enquired about her own day.

Clearly he believed the burden was on Anna to prove her innocence and to justify her disastrous concealment of the facts concerning the loss of her job. Unable to forgive her for withholding so crucial a confidence, Marsh hid his feelings behind a façade of cool civility. Even in his occasional laughter over one or the other of the inconsequential events which amused him, he remained quietly unapproachable. Without trust, he seemed to be saying, she could hardly expect more from him than the pleasant, reserved stranger who confronted her now.

His message was not lost on Anna, who would have preferred a thousand angry quarrels to this hollow mood of deferential calm. But as the days passed she discovered in spite of herself that she too could be proud, and stubborn, and demanding. Reflecting that she had nothing to blame herself for beyond being the victim of a malicious plot against which she could not be expected to defend herself, she reproached Marsh for his blunt disbelief. Not only had he gone behind her back to discover the false charges against her, but he gave them his credence over her own word.

The damning personnel file remained on the coffee table where he had thrown it in his anger. Her glance returned obstinately to it as she paced the apartment. 'What does he expect of me?' she wondered in exasperation. If he believed she was guilty of the crimes alleged in the file, and of marrying him without love, she could hardly expect to convince him he was wrong. Having abandoned his trust in her, he would believe what he chose regardless of whatever action she might take.

But again the thought of her vulnerable friends at N.T.E.L. forced Anna to an effort in which she invested little hope. She put the hated file in an envelope addressed to Charles Robbins, accompanied by a letter explaining that its contents proved there was malice behind her dismissal. Although indifferent to the prospect of regaining her old position, she wrote, she implored Charles to investigate the situation with a view to exposing Porter Deman and protecting his potential victims.

She reasoned that her action must implicitly satisfy Marsh by proving that she did not shrink from defending herself against charges she knew were false. In the improbable event that the company acted upon her request, her name would be cleared. And if, as she bitterly expected, nothing was done, Marsh would have to accept her claim that self-defence was futile against the corporation's inertia and indifference.

But she decided not to tell him of her action until she knew its results. And when her letter went unanswered she shrugged sadly and put it out of her thoughts. What was the point, she wondered, of belabouring a point that was already lost? She had no interest in recapturing the job she had lost, but only in regaining her angry husband's trust. On the other hand, she refused to beg for a confidence she felt she already deserved. Let Marsh himself re-examine his hasty conclusions, she decided resentfully. If she had acted wrongly in hiding her dilemma from him, he had been only too quick to withdraw his support from her. Having rejected her so brutally, he owed her a sign of trust, or even of apology, before expecting her to justify herself anew.

So the stand-off persisted, a marriage between strangers punctuated by bits of insignificant conversation which quickly dissipated into uncomfortable silence. But in the night's quietest hours, as though under cover of a darkness that obscured mistrust and resentment, he came to her, renewing through his caresses a secret contact which persisted underneath the cold civility of the new day.

And thus a pattern was established. Polite strangers by day, Marsh and Anna were impassioned lovers by night. Each time they were intimate, and the heat of his touch stoked daunting fires inside her, she cherished the hope that this closeness promised an end to the discord that troubled their days.

But nothing changed. No matter how early she awoke, he seemed somehow to have arisen and disappeared, as though making a furtive escape from her. His nightly return was hardly an occasion for joyous renewal, since the empty affability of their conversations made her feel lonelier than ever in his company. The evenings passed painfully for Anna, and she went to bed torn by the conflict between her increasing desperation and her secret knowledge that, in the dark of night, she would be his again.

As the days and weeks passed, his lovemaking seemed to take on an infinite variety of meanings. In the absence of real conversation, it was as though all the private feelings which succeed one another during the first weeks of a new marriage were expressing themselves wordlessly through the subtle modulations of his caress, his kiss, the feel of his body.

Sometimes he made love to her with a deliberate violence which seemed to reproach and punish, even as it left her faint with pleasure. At other times his touch was gentle, tender, as though he wished to point out regretfully the bond that still linked him to her, and to strengthen it somehow. Now and then there was a perverse, mocking intimacy in his kisses, a delight in sexual arousal which bypassed trust as it inflamed her shamelessly to him.

And in her own responses to his lovemaking there were a thousand different answers to his unspoken messages. A moan of pleasure on her lips, she would clutch him tightly, and try to pull him closer yet, as though to banish the separation that haunted her. Each time his affection seemed to express a continuing hope for their relationship, she would respond mutely, begging him by her caresses and the little sounds she made to stay with her, not to give up on her.

The entire responsibility for preserving their marriage as a living entity fell on their lovemaking, and never had Anna dreamed that sensual excitement could be so multiple, so marvellous a thing. Yet the passion that bound her to Marsh was not powerful enough to break the silence that tormented her. Each night she knew him a little better, and had a new intuition of what motivated him, hurt him, pleased him. But each day he receded anew into a reserve that her love could not annul.

One morning she found a note on the kitchen table that informed her that Marsh had contacted the University and taken care of Sally's tuition payments for the balance of the year. 'I'll be late tonight,' he added. 'A case.'

His implication was all too clear. He had never relinquished the belief that she had married him for Sally's sake. Well, he would pay, all right, as long as Anna remained home to accept him in her bed at night. He required no real communication beyond that contact. And in order to pay, he must work. She had no right to complain if his case work kept him away until all hours. He was keeping his part of the bargain, wasn't he? Had she not forfeited her rights as a wife when she refused him his right to her confidence?

All too often he called during the day to tell her in blithe tones not to make him a dinner, not to wait up for him. As the weeks passed her loneliness grew more intense, and her own stubborn pride assumed an ever greater place in her thoughts. She could not go on indefinitely in this humiliating position, she told herself. A working woman by inclination, she had no intention of playing the submissive wife for a husband who refused her his respect and attention.

Eventually, she reflected resignedly, this frail skeleton of a marriage must end in separation and divorce. The thought was infinitely saddening, and yet unavoidable. What, then, must be done? Anna's pride told her she must find work. Not only would it obviously be necessary to earn her own living again, at some future date, but she was unwilling to accept this loveless bargain concerning Sally. Let Marsh pay the tuition, then, while there was no alternative. But Anna would somehow find work, without taking the bitter chance of citing N.T.E.L. as a reference, and would eventually pay him back. When it was all over, and she was alone once more, she would look back on this thwarted marriage in terms of expediency. Sally would have been provided for, at the cost of considerable pain and loneliness.

So be it, she decided darkly. Let Marsh's suspicion of her motives become a reality. No longer daring to hope that her relationship with him might be saved, Anna took to the want ads once more, and began looking for work.

CHAPTER EIGHT

'ANNA, *ma chérie*, are you still on nine?' René Lyotard puffed urgently on his strong-smelling French cigarette as he peered between the swinging kitchen doors to the dining room. 'Why don't they leave, for heaven's sake? They got here at six-thirty, and it's almost ten. Oh, *les bougres*, finish your wine and go home!'

'Relax, Marc,' Anna laughed. 'They'll leave. They're enjoying their coffee.'

'You're too understanding, *ma chérie*,' René scowled. 'You were born a saint. But I know you must go home to your husband. And I myself have business tonight. I expect the French to sit up until all hours sipping their brandy, but this is Chicago, *non mais!*'

Anna smiled. René was perpetually excoriating the customers from the safe distance of the kitchen. But as soon as he passed through those swinging doors, he was transformed into the essence of decorous Gallic gallantry.

'*Messieurs, dames,*' he would greet the guests with an easy flourish, 'I welcome you to Ariel. Something to drink before dinner?' Only as he passed Anna on his way to the bar or kitchen would his professional smile fade into a shrug of exasperation.

'*Les gueux!*' he would fume. 'Ariel is the most expensive French restaurant in the city, and our clients are a bunch of peasants who wouldn't know a Camembert from a fireplug. I cannot imitate your natural sweetness, Anna. How you stand them I will never know. It is your superhuman forbearance that gets you such fabulous tips. Not that I begrudge you your success. You deserve it for all you put up with.'

At last the customers stood up to leave. Anna bade them a pleasant good evening and began helping the bus-boy clear the table.

'Anna,' came a stentorian voice from the bar, 'leave that to Henri. May I speak to you for a moment?' Jacques Radier held out his arms lovingly.

'The end of another long day, is it not so, my dear?' he sighed. 'The restaurant business is a demanding one. Now I suppose you will be off to join your lonely husband.'

Anna smiled. 'Actually, I have to meet an old girl friend for a drink, *monsieur*.'

'Oh, *ça alors!*' he threw up his hands. 'Your poor husband must be desperate. Since you agreed to work the dinner hour, the poor man must feel like a bachelor.'

'He's all right,' Anna smiled a trifle ruefully.

'I just wanted to tell you before you leave, Anna, how pleased I am with your work. It is not easy to be the only female *garçon* in a profession dominated by men. But you are doing wonderfully. Even Monsieur Foucault thinks so, and he and I have never agreed on anything in our lives.' He shrugged as he thought of the business partner he could not do without. 'Actually, it is at his suggestion that I wish to ask you something. Your presence has set a sort of tone here at Ariel which seems to be good for business. Roland and I have been thinking that in the role of *hôtesse* you might be even more effective. Not that you are not brilliant at taking care of the tables. What do you think, my dear?'

Anna pursed her lips uncertainly.

'Ah, I know what you are thinking,' he interjected. 'No tips, eh? Well, I can assure you that Roland and I

are thinking in terms of a most substantial salary,
worthy of any well-schooled *maître d'hôtel*. And, of
course, your days of lifting plates of food would be
over.'

'You are very kind, *monsieur*,' Anna smiled. 'I'll be
happy to work in any way you think best.'

'Good,' he beamed. 'Now, you run along, and we'll
talk more of this tomorrow night. *A demain, mon petit.*'

As she said goodnight to her colleagues and
prepared to walk out into the freezing November
wind, Anna reflected that Monsieur Radier's proposal
might be a good idea. Perhaps a job as hostess would
be less exhausting.

Anna had grown to love her work at Ariel since the
day Messrs. Foucault and Radier had decided, not
without reservations, to hire her in spite of her
inexperience. She had given no references, claiming
that economic hard times were forcing her to go to
work to supplement her husband's income. She had
not held a job, she said, since before her college
education.

Her new employers had shrugged indifferently at
her explanation, for they were concerned only with
restaurant experience, of which she had none, and
preferred to train her themselves in any case. Despite
their irascible treatment of each other, both were fond
of Anna, and made every effort to make her first weeks
of work as easy as possible.

To their surprise and delight, Anna seemed to have
been born with the instinctive tact and delicacy
required of a highly trained waiter. The aura of quiet
friendliness she brought to Ariel seemed to make the
customers happy, and she found herself greeted
warmly by increasingly familiar faces as the weeks
went by. Her slim good looks were not without their
favourable effect as well, and more than once she

caught a glimpse of a happy client pointing her out with words of praise to one or the other of her bosses.

The pleasure of doing a job well after the idleness enforced by the collapse of her first career was encouraging. And the banter she enjoyed with René and the other waiters made Anna feel she belonged to a hardworking, if somewhat excitable, team of professionals linked by common needs and ambitions. Her busy nights at Ariel took her mind off the continuing estrangement that troubled her marriage to Marsh. She returned home each night with a welcome sense of accomplishment that took the edge off the feelings of failure which haunted her personal life.

Marsh, for his part, had initially said little in response to the news of her new job. Apparently indifferent to the use to which she put her time when she was not with him, he continued devoting long hours to his own work. Although Anna thought she sensed a touch of pride in her energy and initiative on his part, the intuition was soon eclipsed by the pained silence which hung over so many of her hours with him. And so she clung to the excitement of her work as the only bright light in what was sure to be her future life alone.

But marriage to Marsh Hamilton, she discovered, was never as predictable as it might seem, regardless of the mutual stubbornness which seemed to poison her relationship with him. For with studied casualness, during the moments of fleeting reconciliation or mere relaxation which overtook them both, he drew her out gently on her thoughts about the rigours of her new profession and the personalities of her surprisingly accommodating bosses.

'Who runs the cash register at Ariel?' he enquired one evening.

'Madame Foucault,' Anna replied. 'Why do you ask?'

'I wondered whether it was a woman,' he said. 'In France, no matter how fancy the establishment, the *caissière* will always be a woman. The men are trusted to handle the tables, charm the clients and cook the food, but when it comes to the francs the woman is boss.'

'Come to think of it,' Anna laughed, 'Madame Foucault does act the part. Her husband is quite the tyrant when she's not around, but he turns into a puppydog when she comes into view.'

'Perhaps the French have a point,' said Marsh. 'A lot of the businessmen I come into contact with have mucked up their books so badly that they have to pay their accountants more than their creditors.'

'If that's the way you feel about it,' Anna smiled with a touch of complacency, 'you'll be happy to know that when Madame Foucault is indisposed, her job falls to yours truly.'

'You're kidding,' he said, quirking an eyebrow in surprise.

'And not only that,' she added, 'I'm the one who takes Ariel's receipts to the bank in the afternoon.'

'Well, aren't you the unpredictable one,' he smiled. 'So much responsibility already. Aren't you afraid a mugger will assault you for the money, even in that fancy neighbourhood?'

'If that happened,' Anna bristled, 'I'd simply hit him with the bank's money sack—it weighs a ton.'

'I believe you would,' he nodded. 'With that stubborn streak of yours, you'd be a dangerous enemy when roused.'

And he fell silent, his evocation of the independence he had admired in Anna before their marriage no doubt warring with his continuing distrust. For her part Anna could not help feeling satisfied to report her employers' implicit confidence in her to the man who so rigidly withheld his own. At the same time she was aware that through his casual questions, so bland in appearance, he was subtly learning more about her in spite of the silent gulf that persisted between them. Uncomfortably she asked herself whether his inquisititiveness bespoke a remnant of commitment to her. Perhaps, in his grudging way, he still considered himself her husband, and wished to express his support through friendly conversation.

On the other hand, she wondered bitterly, perhaps his occasional interest was born of morbid curiosity about the private life he thought she wished to conceal from him. Perhaps he was interrogating her with an eye to preventing further unbidden revelations about her activities from strangers. The inscrutable silence which so often reigned in his demeanour hardly betokened trust or affection.

Let him think what he liked, Anna decided with a shrug. She herself knew how trustworthy she was, and the steady progress of her new career came as no surprise to her. When the time came her initiative would see her through, notwithstanding Marsh's feelings about her.

The cocktail lounge where Debby Johnson awaited was only two and a half blocks away, but Anna could not suppress a sigh of fatigue as she hurried through Ariel's front door. She felt unusually tired today. Last night was her night off from work, and she had had to accompany Marsh to a party at the District Attorney's house, and had not slept until after one o'clock in the morning. Apparently embarrassed at Anna's invisibility to his colleagues since their marriage, Marsh had wanted her to put in an appearance, since his partners and friends were bringing their spouses.

Perhaps, Anna wondered, there might be talk about the wife Marsh left alone during the late hours he worked. She had agreed to go along, in spite of the alienation she felt from her husband and his world. Her job had gone a long way towards assuaging her loneliness and restoring her sense of independence, and she was beginning to face the eventuality of a separation from Marsh with some courage.

'Why don't you wear my favourite dress?' he had asked as she stood in her bathrobe before the limited array of garments in her closet.

'Marsh, no!' she had protested, her eyes darting to the silken contours of the dress on its hanger. Sinuously low-cut in pearl white with slender shoulder straps, it was the most daringly feminine of her evening dresses. 'It's too . . .'

'Sexy?' he asked with a grin.

'Well, yes,' she admitted. 'I don't think the occasion is right for it.'

'I do,' he said. 'I want to show you off.'

'You're kidding,' she said ruefully. 'That sounds funny coming from you.'

'I don't see why you say that,' he commented.

'I haven't had the impression that you were exactly bursting with pride in me,' she returned.

'Ah-hah,' he drawled, his long arms encircling her from behind. 'You're breaking the lawyer's first law: never assume. Never try to read someone's mind without knowing the facts beforehand. Remember?'

Anna made no response, for the warm touch of his hard body against her back, so intoxicating in its sheer virility, made it difficult for her to concentrate on his teasing words.

'I have many reasons for pride in you,' Marsh murmured against her earlobe. 'Not the least of which is the sight of those long legs in a clinging dress. Why shouldn't I share the pleasure with my overworked colleagues? I won't be jealous.'

'Mmm,' she sighed, too bewitched by his exploring lips and by the hands that had slipped to the curve of her thighs to regret that his compliment was so insubstantial. If he was sincere about having pride in her, he would surely have better reasons than the mere shape of her body.

'I wonder if the D.A. would notice our arriving late,' he whispered seductively into her ear. 'I'm no longer thinking of the dress, but of what goes into it. We don't have to leave yet.'

'Yes, we do,' she sighed. 'We're expected. You owe him the courtesy after all your years with him.'

'When he gets a look at you, he'll understand why I was late.'

'Thanks,' she said, extricating herself from his embrace with a difficulty made greater by her own reluctance. 'But no, thanks. I don't want to cause you embarrassment in front of your friends.'

'No danger of that,' said Marsh, his appraising eyes taking in the contours of her slender limbs under the bathrobe.

And yet embarrassed indifference seemed exactly his attitude after their arrival at the party, for he seemed eager to shun Anna from the moment his onetime boss ushered them into his enormous living room. The faces of the lawyers and judges were unfamiliar, and Anna found it difficult to make conversation with them. They all seemed so tall, so confident, so successful . . . And they talked endlessly about subjects Anna was virtually ignorant of.

Marsh was anything but helpful in the circumstances. After hurriedly introducing her to a host of strangers whose names she forgot in spite of herself, he disappeared into a den where some close friends from his days as a prosecutor were engaged in jocular conversation about the city's current political struggles. It soon became clear to Anna that he had no intention of emerging, so she did her best to keep up her end of one casual exchange after another as the evening dragged by.

More than a few guests had already left, their overcoats securely buttoned in anticipation of the frigid wind outside, when Anna at last decided to seek Marsh out.

Already tired, she gently suggested that it was time to go home. But Marsh would not hear of it. His levity among his friends seemed to underscore his alienation from Anna, for she had not heard him laugh so heartily since her honeymoon with him.

He was seated on a couch surrounded by young lawyers. Among them was a stunningly beautiful blonde woman whom Anna heard addressed as May. Dressed in a clinging skirt and blouse which accentuated her healthy, sleek curves, May was astonishingly attractive. Her long hair bore the traces of the summer sun's bleaching, and her limpid blue eyes darted intelligently from one young lawyer to another. She seemed quite at home among her male colleagues, and laughed easily at their jokes. At the same time, Anna had the impression that May was quite aware her beauty made her the centre of attraction wherever she went, and frankly enjoyed the attention.

For a long moment Marsh did not look up to see that his wife had come into the room. Someone was making a joke, and Marsh added a clever rejoinder which made everyone laugh. With a touch of discomfort Anna saw May place her slender hand on Marsh's arm in a gesture of camaraderie which seemed to conceal a grain of possessiveness.

Marsh introduced her as May Reynolds.

'She's beautiful,' Anna observed later, as they drove home.

'May? Yes, I guess so,' he agreed absently. 'She's a damned good lawyer, very aggressive. She'll be a D.A. herself one day, I'll bet.'

Aggressive in more ways than one, Anna thought, but resisted the temptation to mention that May had been flirting with Marsh. Seeing his preoccupied face behind the wheel of the car, she realised he had withdrawn from her once more. With an inner sigh, she reflected that it made little difference to her marriage if other women courted Marsh's attentions. There was not much affection left in him to be alienated, and the marriage itself would not last long.

Tonight Marsh would be late, as usual, so Anna had accepted Debby's invitation to have a drink after work and talk over old times. The two women had not seen each other since Anna's marriage, and neither wanted to stay out of touch too long, since the friendship they had developed at N.T.E.L. was important to both.

'Anna!' Debby exclaimed as the door closed on the night wind. 'How are you, kid? Gosh, it's been a long time!'

'I'm frozen at the moment, to tell you the truth,' said Anna.

'Come on, then,' Debby smiled. 'Let's get ourselves a hot buttered rum or something.'

'How's Barbara?' asked Anna as they sat in a booth towards the rear of the lounge.

'Oh, you know,' Debby sighed. 'The same.'

'Really?' Anna asked miserably. 'Oh, no!' As the waiter took their order, she thought with quiet horror of the situation at N.T.E.L.

'Debby,' she said at length, 'I feel like such a

coward. To think that Barbara is still suffering from
that . . .'

'Never mind, Anna,' said Debby. 'You did all you
could, and it didn't do any good. There's nothing to
blame yourself for.'

'Yes, there is,' Anna insisted, thinking ruefully of
Marsh's legal estimation of the situation. 'I should
never have let the whole sordid mess run its course
behind closed doors. If I'd taken legal action in my
own behalf, the spotlight would have been on Deman.
As it is, he goes along with impunity . . . It's
infuriating!'

'Don't blame yourself, Anna, You had to get on
with your own life. Don't forget, you were the victim,
not the criminal.'

Anna had to suppress a wry smile at her friend's
words. In recent weeks she had so accustomed herself
to feelings of guilt over her misfortune that it was
difficult to recall her innocence.

'I don't know if you knew,' Debby interjected, 'that
Barbara tried to help you. She went to see Robbins
when you were fired. Obviously it didn't make any
difference.'

Anna shook her head, contemplating the extent of
the damage Porter Deman had done in her life—
damage of which Debby could have no inkling,
ignorant as she was of the existence of the damning
personnel file and Marsh's discovery of it.

'Well,' Debby concluded with an ironic smile, 'at
least Deman hasn't got around to me. If he does, he'll
get a surprise, I can promise you! I may get fired, but
I'll leave him something to remember me by. Maybe a
split lip or a bloody nose.'

She fell silent for a moment as steaming glasses of
hot rum were placed on the table between them.

'As a matter of fact,' she went on when the waiter

had gone, 'we haven't been seeing much of him recently. There's a new girl there now. She's probably getting all his attentions.'

As the glow faded from Anna's cheeks in the warm air, Debby looked concernedly at her.

'You look pale, Anna. Have you been ill?' she asked.

'No,' Anna replied. 'A little tired, I suppose. My job keeps me hopping.'

'How is marriage agreeing with you?' Debby pursued, obviously concealing her concern.

'All right,' Anna answered evasively.

'I still can't believe it. I got a look at Marsh when he was at N.T.E.L. How handsome can a man get!' Debby exclaimed. 'I'm so happy for you, kid. You deserve someone like him. And I guess he came along at the right time.'

'Yes,' Anna agreed, inwardly weighing the absurdity of her words, 'I suppose he did.' She dared not reveal to her friend that her troubles at N.T.E.L. had managed to compromise what had seemed an ideal marriage. If Marsh had entered her life at any other time, her relationship with him would have eluded the rocks on which it was foundering now. Instead, she had met him in the very corridors of N.T.E.L.

'If you don't mind my saying so,' said Debby, her brow furrowed in concern, 'you look downright unhappy, Anna. Are you sure you're all right?'

'Yes,' Anna sighed. 'I'm okay. Don't worry about me, Deb. I'm just trying to get myself straightened out. The last two months have been . . . well, hectic.'

'Marriage is quite a step, I guess,' Debby observed. 'Of course,' she smirked, 'I wouldn't know, since I haven't been proposed to lately. Or even propositioned.'

With a grateful smile Anna contemplated her friend's accustomed humour. Its self-denigrating aspect never troubled Debby's close friends, for they knew her relative lack of sex appeal was more than compensated for by her irrepressible personality. The dignity and self-respect underlying her jokes at her own expense were never out of sight, and she herself seemed confident that she was not destined for a spinster's life.

'I imagine,' she probed diffidently, 'that a big strong guy like Marsh can be stubborn about what he wants.'

Anna nodded, uncomfortably aware that the other girl's guess was close to the truth.

'So can I,' she smiled. After all, she had her own rigidity to blame as much as that of her wilful husband for her current problems.

'My mother always used to say that one has to let a man have his own way—or at least let him think he does,' Debby laughed. 'Otherwise his pride will make him impossible to live with. Be patient, she'd say, and bide your time until he comes around to your way of thinking. Of course, she was talking over her head, because my father was always impossible, and still is.'

'Maybe he would have been more impossible,' Anna smiled, 'if she hadn't been diplomatic.'

'You could be right about that.' Debby's sparkling eyes were fixed affectionately on her friend. 'But I could never be as passive as she was. When and if I ever get married, I'll probably bring all kinds of trouble down on myself by opening my big mouth when I should be keeping it shut.'

'Nonsense,' said Anna. 'You'll be perfect.' Uncomfortably she reflected that her case was the opposite. It was her silence that Marsh could not forgive.

'Now that you're on the other side of the line,' Debby said in a confidential tone, 'can you tell an amateur like me what it's like? I mean, is it hard to get used to living with a man?'

'Now look who's being diplomatic!' Anna laughed. 'I'll be honest with you, Deb. Marsh is a wonderful man, and I love him. Nevertheless, we're having problems. Sometimes I think it's all my own fault, and sometimes I'm just not sure of anything.'

'That's not possible,' Debby remonstrated. 'I know you, Anna. You're not the type to ruin a good thing.'

'That's what I would have thought,' Anna sighed, 'until this whole . . . this trouble started. The terrible part is that it hardly has anything to do with us—I mean, with our real relationship. I think I belong with Marsh, but we just can't seem to . . . to . . .' She shook her head. 'I'm talking in circles, aren't I? I suppose I just can't bear to go into the details.'

'Don't, then,' Debby smiled. 'I didn't mean to pry. I mean,' she added with a laugh, 'I did mean to pry, but it's none of my business. But look at it this way, Anna: you're still together, aren't you? You're both still committed to each other.'

For how long? Anna wondered miserably while doing her best to return her friend's optimistic smile.

'I know I shouldn't talk,' Debby went on, 'but give it time, Anna. It will work itself out eventually. Just don't give up prematurely. I saw the way Marsh looked at you at N.T.E.L. If a man ever looked at me that way, I'd drop dead of surprise. I know he feels deeply for you.'

Grateful for Debby's well-meaning support, Anna squeezed her hand. She only wished she could take her encouraging words to heart. But there was no forgetting the fragile state of her imperilled marriage.

'I hope you're right,' she said. 'Perhaps somehow things will work out.'

'Just remember, Anna: if you ever need anything,

any help or anything, you know where to come. Okay?'

'Okay,' agreed Anna, allowing herself to hope that there was a grain of truth in Debby's assessment of her situation. After all, she reasoned uncertainly, she and Marsh were not separated yet. Despite the bitter gulf between them, they remained married. Perhaps that fact counted for something . . .

Debby's smile disappeared suddenly as she peered behind Anna to the entrance to the lounge.

'Listen,' she whispered. 'Don't turn around. I think I just saw Marsh come in.'

Anna turned paler than before. 'Is he . . .?'

'He's with someone. That's funny . . .' Debby's brow furrowed in perplexity.

Anna could not suppress her curiosity a second longer. Turning in her seat, she saw Marsh helping a woman off with her coat by a booth near the door. His companion's back was turned, but her lovely blonde hair left little doubt as to her identity. A glance in the mirror behind the bar confirmed Anna's suspicion. Marsh was with May Reynolds.

Possessed suddenly of a strange alertness, Anna scanned the walls behind Debby. There was a back entrance.

'I'm going to have to go,' she said quickly, pulling on her coat.

'Anna . . .' Debby's eyes glowed with pained sympathy.

'It's all right,' said Anna, squeezing her hand. 'It's not what it seems. He works with her. But I really don't want to see them right now. Keep in touch, all right?'

Debby smiled, although her features were still clouded by a perplexity which Anna was in too great a hurry to notice.

'Take care,' she said. 'Call me.'

The night wind bit savagely through her coat as she hurried towards the subway. Although Marsh's apartment building was only a pleasant walk away from Ariel in warm weather, the winter wind forced Anna to take the one-stop subway ride home.

She stood on the warm platform in an agony of chagrin and conflicting thoughts. Poor Debby! She would certainly arrive at a conclusion less innocent than Anna's assurances indicated. How embarrassing it all was! Certainly, Marsh did work with May Reynolds in an indirect way, and there was nothing so terrible in buying her a drink before saying goodnight. But the look in May's eyes at the District Attorney's party had indicated anything but indifference towards Marsh.

May might well be perfectly aware that Marsh worked long hours and spent little time with his wife. She might suspect that his marriage was in trouble, and have an interest in being as friendly as possible, in anticipation of the day when he would be free again.

To think that, if it had not been for that rear entrance, Anna might have been forced to greet them, to introduce Debby, to converse with them. The embarrassment would have been too much to bear. Everyone would have seen her confusion . . .

The train roared deafeningly through the tunnel and screeched to a stop. Anna boarded it and sat down, although she knew she would have to stand up in thirty seconds and prepare to mount the long flights of stairs to the street.

There was no denying it—May Reynolds was a very sexy and attractive young woman. Anna recalled the alert cleverness in May's eyes last night. She was obviously intelligent. And right now she was sitting in a cosy booth with Marsh, chatting about work, perhaps about some mutual interest. Anna had felt May's gaze scan her critically at the party. How uncomfortable it would have felt, she thought, to be appraised competitively by those pretty blue eyes tonight, if she had not made her escape through the back door.

'Made my escape,' Anna thought with an angry shudder as she rushed headlong through the wind towards home. She could not bear the passivity enforced upon her by the predicament that had begun at N.T.E.L. Although she had acted with courageous directness in her responses to Porter Deman, to Charles Robbins, and even to Marsh, she somehow kept finding herself in the position of a furtive, shamefaced victim. She had had quite enough of concealing embarrassing truths, avoiding confrontations, and fearing the actions of others.

Somehow she must regain her independence, however lonely that prospect was.

She had saved most of the money she had earned at Ariel. Before long she would be in a position to strike out on her own. Her new career put the N.T.E.L. disaster behind her. If she continued to save scrupulously, she would be able to pay Marsh back for Sally's tuition. Then there would be only the future to consider. A future without entanglements, without guilt . . . Without love, perhaps, but a person could become used to living without a lot of things.

Anna had just stepped out of a hot, bracing shower and was combing her wet hair before the bathroom mirror when she heard Marsh's key in the door. As she stood in the steamy air, regarding her own unhappy face in the mirror, the quiet sounds of his habitual night-time activity filtered into the room. The closet door opened and closed; ice clinked in a glass; a rustle came from the bedroom as he changed his clothes. The phonograph in the living room was turned on as he picked out one of the quiet classical records he used as tranquillisers after a hard day's work. As usual, he didn't bother to greet her.

The pathos of standing alone in the bathroom while her estranged husband went about his solitary business only a few feet away seemed suddenly unbearable to Anna.

'This has got to stop,' she thought. The scene she had witnessed in the cocktail lounge, while perhaps not so significant in itself, was the last straw for this troubled marriage. She could no longer bear the expression of intense pain that clouded the green eyes in the mirror. Deciding not to bother blow-drying her hair, she moved deliberately towards the living room.

Marsh was sitting in a chair, wearing jeans and the white shirt he had worn to work. His eyes were closed. The muted strains of a string quartet filled the room with polite restraint. She sat down uncomfortably on the couch opposite him.

'Can I talk to you?' she asked.

'Oh, hi,' he said with an amiability that seemed feigned. His eyes remained closed. 'I thought you might have gone to bed.'

Anna remained silent for a moment, reflecting bitterly that he would not even have said hello had she not spoken to him first.

At last he opened his eyes and regarded her quizzically.

'What's on your mind?' he asked.

'Us,' she said simply.

'What do you mean, "us"?'

'I mean the fact that there isn't any more us,' she said.

'I don't get it,' he sighed irritably, closing his eyes again.

'I think you'd better open your eyes, Marsh,' she said angrily.

'All right, all right,' he sighed, misunderstanding her. 'What is it you want, Anna? I'm tired.'

'So am I. Tired of this whole mess we're in.'

A long silence ensued as they both considered the import of her words. For nearly two months this day had been approaching, and had weighed upon their routine of silent co-existence.

'What do you propose?' he asked with studied calm.

She took a deep breath. 'Divorce,' she said. 'Right away.'

Again Marsh was silent. Although Anna was glad her thought was out in the open, the sound of the word terrified her. These last unhappy weeks had convinced her that her marriage was failing, but had also made it painfully clear that its definitive end would leave indelible scars.

'Is there someone else?' he asked, opening his eyes.

His egotism dumbfounded her. Had he assumed his lovemaking was so bewitching that she would live in total silence with him until another man came along? With an effort she ignored his question and searched for words which would describe her thoughts dispassionately.

'I mean,' he went on cruelly, 'who would take care of your sister? Without me in the picture?'

'I'll take care of Sally myself, thank you,' she began. 'And as for there being someone else, Marsh, I don't think people who live in glass houses should throw stones.'

'What's that supposed to mean?'

'There's no one else in *my* life,' she said, her voice trembling with anger. 'Can you say the same?'

He stared at her in perplexity. 'I'd like to know what the hell you're talking about,' he said darkly.

'I'm talking about the woman I saw you with tonight,' she said.

His face clouded with growing anger.

'Don't try to deny it,' she added, struggling to suppress the fear his look inspired in her.

A dry, menacing smile curled his lip.

'Have you been spying on me, love?' he asked.

'Not at all,' she answered. 'If I'd wanted to spy on you, I probably would have found out unpleasant things a long time ago. I met Debby Johnson for a drink tonight, and there you were.'

Marsh frowned. 'I really don't understand you,' he said. 'Are you talking about May?'

'Who do you think I'm talking about?'

He smiled ironically. 'I think that job of yours, or something, I don't know what, is going to your head, Anna. There's nothing between me and May Reynolds. We're working together. That's all there is to it.'

'That may be your idea of the relationship, but I doubt that she shares it. If, that is, you're telling me the truth.'

'Don't talk to me about truth, Anna,' he growled. 'You wouldn't know it if you tripped over it.'

'Don't try to evade the question!' she snapped.

'My God,' he laughed bitterly. 'You're really full of surprises. One never knows what to expect from you. I never thought you were the jealous type.'

Anna lapsed into frustrated silence. Why, after all, should she be disturbed about Marsh's relationship with May Reynolds? The failure of their marriage had nothing to do with infidelity. In some corner of her mind, Anna herself must be harbouring an involuntary grain of possessiveness towards the man with whom she lived in such torment.

'Well,' he went on blithely, 'I suppose I can indulge your mania, since it means nothing to me. The fact is that we're involved with the D.A. on a difficult and rather exciting case at the moment, and my work brings me into contact with May. I buy her a drink sometimes, at the end of the day, or she buys me one. The lounge where you saw us is near my office and her field location. We're regulars there.'

'What difference does that make?' asked Anna.

'I see,' he said, the same sardonic smile curling his lip. 'I forgot my vocation. Every lawyer knows that the jealous mind will put a negative construction on anything at all. You know, Anna, jealousy is a real sickness. It can be treated.'

'Don't talk down to me!' she shot back. 'I've seen the way she looks at you!'

A short, sarcastic laugh escaped him. 'Women,' he said.

'I wouldn't attribute my point of view to my sex, if I were you,' warned Anna, feeling herself flush angrily at his condescension. 'At least I haven't ordered her personnel file from the District Attorney in order to investigate her past!'

He shrugged. 'You're hopeless,' he sighed. 'What difference should it make to you, anyway? I like having a drink with May. She's cute, and fairly witty. Besides, I'm lonely. You're never at home, since you're always working nights. Why shouldn't I have a little amusement?'

'That sounds funny coming from you,' Anna said bitterly. 'You're the one who's never home. My work is the only distraction I get.'

'And speaking of personnel files,' he added, ignoring her words, 'I think an investigation such as the one you suggest would show that our May has nothing to hide. I'll say one thing for her: she's a very straightforward woman.'

'Good for her,' Anna retorted. 'She sounds well suited to you. Perhaps you can take a more permanent interest in her after we separate.'

'I doubt it,' he drawled. 'May has a good head on her shoulders, but she's a bit too candid. Never holds anything back. Wears her heart on her sleeve. No, Anna, she's just not my type. I like a woman with a little mystery.'

'You're fooling yourself, Marsh,' Anna snapped, her growing anger fueled by weeks of resentment. 'Any mystery you might have attached to me has been of your own imagining. I told you the whole truth about myself long ago. If you want to see a mind that gets pleasure out of putting suspicious constructions on everything, just look in the mirror.'

'I don't think so,' he contradicted her blithely. 'It seems to me that everyone who comes in contact with you has some inkling of your aversion to the truth. For instance, your current employers at the restaurant— are they aware that you used to work at N.T.E.L.? How about your old friend Debby? Does she know why you're working outside your old career? And, of course, there's always me. Why, if I weren't a lawyer, and trained to put two and two together, I wouldn't even realise you sent your famous personnel file back to your old Vice-President.'

'So,' Anna fumed, 'you haven't changed your ways. You're still spying on me.'

'Not at all,' he said mockingly. 'Just using the things I already know to speculate on what's going on behind my back. After all, I'm not in the habit of expecting you to keep me informed.'

'Why should I?' she rejoined. 'Whatever I might say would be greeted with disbelief.'

'You have a point there.'

Anna avoided his mocking gaze, her eyes scanning the cityscape outside the windows. Struck dumb by his cruel words, she fought to control her emotions.

'In all these weeks,' she said at length, 'you've never forgiven me for something that wasn't even my fault. You have no pity, Marsh.'

'I wouldn't say that,' Marsh shook his head with infuriating suavity. 'I do pity you, Anna. I simply live with you in the only reasonable manner. In a way, I'm the perfect husband for you. A good lawyer is trained to take what people tell him with a grain of salt. He proceeds on the assumption that everyone has something to hide. Since you're a person of whom that is true to an exaggerated degree, I can relate to you quite well by simply assuming that whatever you tell me conceals something unspoken.'

'Wonderful,' Anna snapped. 'I'm glad I'm good for something, even if only for sharpening your professional instincts.'

'The day I proposed to you,' Marsh went on, 'I said you were a woman who needed watching. I had no idea how right I was.'

'I don't think I'll be needing your surveillance any longer, Marsh. To be quite frank, I've had enough of you and your reproaches and your silence. Once you're free, you're welcome to seek out another mysterious woman, if that's what gives you a thrill. Personally, I don't care what you do.'

'I'm grateful for your blessing,' he mocked. 'But I won't hear any talk of divorce. Not now, anyway.'

'Why not?' she asked. 'You yourself admit that our marriage isn't working, that it's a mistake.'

'Not working, I'll agree,' he said. 'A mistake? I'm not sure. Time will tell. There may be residual benefits to a life without trust. You've forfeited your right to any confidence I might have in you, but there's always this, my love.' He rose abruptly from his chair. 'You're still my type.'

A mischievous grin curled his lips as he advanced towards her. Suddenly Anna realised she was dressed only in her robe. Before she could move to defend herself, he had crossed the carpet in one lithe stride and curled his arm around her back.

'You're good-looking,' he said harshly into her ear. 'You're very sexy, in your own way.' His powerful arms held her like an iron vice, and he pressed himself brutally to her.

'Why consider a divorce?' he said, his hands beginning to caress her back, her hips. 'We have a good time together in bed, don't we? And your sister is taken care of, isn't she? And I only ask one thing of you, don't I?' His questions were like little contemptuous slaps which wounded her pride, even as his hands and lips quickened her pulse with tiny spasms of growing desire.

'Your part of the bargain isn't all that bad, is it?' he whispered, his lips caressing the tender hollow of her neck. 'You've got your job, your independence, your privacy. And when the witching hour arrives,' he added, his muscular chest grazing the taut tips of her breasts, 'I give you a pretty good time.'

Anna wanted to cry out, to push him away, and never to forgive him for the humiliation he was inflicting upon her. But already her treacherous body. tingling with insidious sensations, responded to his seductive touch with a shudder he was all too quick to interpret correctly. Glorying in his ability to arouse her against her own better judgment, Marsh laughed against her flesh.

'A bargain is a bargain, my love,' he murmured. 'Why not let yourself go, and enjoy the benefits?'

From the depths of her memory the echo of Porter

Deman's cruel words resonated forth to join those of Marsh. It was the same cruelty, the same joy in prostituting her, in coveting her body at the expense of her self-respect. '*Why don't you let yourself go . . .?*'

With an athletic quickness that took him by surprise she whirled in his grasp and slapped his face with all her might. For an instant his black eyes gleamed dangerously down at her. Then, with amused admiration for her aggressiveness, he grasped her more firmly.

His lips claimed her own with brutal intimacy, and she heard herself gasp in consternation at her own excitement. His hands had stolen expertly under the fabric of her robe to explore her nakedness, their subtle, knowing movements driving her to fearsome heights of desire. Slowly, with powerful expertise, his arms manipulated the weight of her body, shifting its centre of gravity, now supporting, now letting go, so that she was lowered naked to the carpet, as vulnerable as an insect around which a spider spins its imprisoning web. And all the while Marsh's deep, probing kiss held her in rapt immobility as he stripped off the last shreds of fabric separating her from him.

In a trice he had slipped out of his own clothes, without releasing her from the intoxicating, stunning contact of his body. She felt sullied to her depths, mocked by his arrogant sensuality, degraded by the disrespect with which he had stripped her, pulled her to the floor. What made it all worse was that in his perverse triumph over her unavailing resistance, he felt and knew the strength of the tie that still bound her to him.

She could feel an invisible smirk of victory in the very movements of his limbs as her lips returned his kiss, her flesh burned against his own, and a little groan of helpless pleasure stirred in her throat.

Without haste he prepared to come to her, for her body's shuddering responses made it clear she was ready to accept him, right here on the carpet, in the warm, still air. A hand rested confidently on her breast, the palm a mocking touch against the poised hardness of the nipple. He brushed the sleek flesh of her stomach with a kiss that sent a great shiver of yielding through her. His hand closed over her shoulder, pinning her to the floor like a living, breathing doll, an inanimate object brought to sensual life by his touch.

As she felt the hardness of his body settle luxuriantly over her, she decided to let him have his way without a struggle. She would oppose her passive resistance to his selfish pleasure, spoiling through her pliant coldness the intimacy he sought. But it was no use, for already her nerves tingled with involuntary delight at the warm, sliding touch of his skin on her own.

So she gave up all resistance, and accepted her role as his prostitute, the plaything of his desire. A perverse little voice whose echo stole over her throbbing flesh told her to enjoy herself, to sink into this sensual mire of humiliation, to allow herself to be titillated by the novelty of this experience, by this delight in sex without love. And perhaps her very acquiescence would punish him, she thought vaguely, for he would know that she also could take pleasure in his hard body without asking or receiving any human tenderness from him.

But her resentful thoughts were brushed away like gossamer in the wind by the tumult of involuntary ecstasy which overcame her. The last remnants of her self-respect seemed borne into oblivion as Marsh held her tighter, closer, as her traitorous body arched shamelessly and pressed itself against him, languid, delighting—and all gave way suddenly, all burst and relaxed into a wave of overwhelming passion. He had had his way, for he knew her too intimately to be checked by her defences.

And even now, lying faint in his arms, her eyes closed, Anna looked inside herself for the unforgiving woman who must live without him forever, and it was his black eyes that seemed to look out at her, holding her imperiously with their penetrating gaze.

She stood before the mirror, combing the tangles of sensual rapture out of her hair, having washed the traces of Marsh's assault from her body. He was in bed, reading. The eyes in the glass were tormented, exhausted. Her reserves of initiative seemed at a low ebb, and she felt defeat in every corner of her soul. There had been no love in his touch tonight. He had somehow extinguished it through the cold force of his resentment. And her will had reached its final paralysis, for her senses had actually delighted in being sullied by him.

In her cheeks she saw the pallor that Debby had noticed. Anna alone had suspected the real reason for the changes her body had undergone recently. Tomorrow or the next day she would know the results of the tests. If it was true, she was lost. Pregnancy would mean the end of life as she had known it, and the beginning of a time whose perils she could not even imagine. Married without trust, a mother without a real husband . . .

But why worry about the future? It would only be more of the same. Time seemed to have ground to a halt, stopping in one hollow instant which spread and expanded, consuming past and future alike. Only this awful unhappiness remained, diffusing itself like a gas,

filling up the world, leaving no air to breathe. To
think of repairing the damage caused by these weeks of
angry silence was a futile thing now. She herself no
longer trusted the husband whose confidence she had
lost long ago.

There was nothing left but to go on, to endure. Let
him enjoy her body, then. If it pleased him, let him
have his way. She might as well enjoy him, too.

Or leave him, she thought as her mind jumped from
one extreme to another. Go back to living alone, and
working at Ariel. Raising her ... her baby. Could it
be? She was to telephone the doctor's nurse tomorrow.
Her mind burned with an anticipation from which all
joy and courage had been banished.

The pale face in the mirror swung and disappeared
as she turned towards the bedroom.

CHAPTER NINE

'MRS HAMILTON, is it?'

'That's right.'

'Can you hold the line a moment? I believe we have the test result.'

Anna sat in anxious silence in the empty living room, her eyes darting sightlessly across the urban horizon outside the window. No sound came across the line; the nurse must have put her on an electronic hold.

With a shudder she glanced at the space of carpet beside the couch. Only last night Marsh had taken her there, brutally, abruptly, without affection. And now she was to find out whether she carried a new life in her body. The strain of the contradiction between the pain of her marriage and the joy of childbearing seemed intolerable. How could she presume to bring a new baby into the world, when her own life was in chaos? A child needs security, and that can only come from a strong relationship between its parents. Without that bond of understanding between mother and father, the infant would be little better than an orphan.

There was only one way out. A single parent would be better than two parents who were at each other's throats . . .

'Hello? Mrs Hamilton?'

'Yes.'

'Well, we have the result, and it's positive.'

There was a silence as Anna tried to cope with the reality announced by the voice on the line.

'Are you happy with the result, I hope?' The nurse's voice was hesitant, friendly.

'Oh ... yes,' Anna assured her, 'of course I am. Thank you very much.'

Placing the receiver gingerly on the phone, as if afraid to upset some invisible balance of nature at this critical moment, she closed her eyes and took a few deep breaths.

A child! She was to be a mother. For a brief, wonderful moment the thought of the gentle, tiny life within her body banished all other ideas. Whatever the tribulations she had endured these past months and years, only a few months now separated her from the miracle of bringing into the world a tiny boy or girl destined to grow into a real person. A separate personality, possessed of its own unknowable destiny, and yet bearing the wonderful and mysterious traces of the parents who created it. Whom would it resemble? Would it be a boy or a girl? What would be the sound of its little voice as it grew? What would be its interests? Anna's mind was thronged by all the joyful thoughts that come with a first pregnancy.

She stood up and walked the apartment aimlessly. As the couch, the bedroom passed before her eyes, her happiness began to give way to the desperate thoughts brought on by last night's scene with Marsh. Clearly he had lost what remained of his respect for her. He had treated her like a sexual slave. She shuddered anew as she recalled the echo of Porter Deman's cruel, manipulative words on Marsh's own lips. Never had she dreamed him capable of such arrogant cruelty.

She had endured these many weeks of silence in the waning hope that the resentment poisoning her marriage would dissipate with the passage of time. But it had obviously grown worse. Marsh left no doubt that he neither expected nor intend to give real love to his future relationship with Anna. As far as he was concerned, his worst suspicions of her own motives in marrying him had become the only reality of their life together. It was a marriage of convenience, cemented only by mutual self-interest. The blitheness with which he welcomed this existence without affection or trust had been the final blow to Anna's hopes.

It had been one thing to contemplate a divorce for the simple reason that life with Marsh was unhappy. It was quite another to imagine this loveless arrangement as a basis for bringing up a vulnerable child. Marsh's arrogant refusal to consider a separation could no longer be taken seriously. Anna's pregnancy lent a new urgency to the situation.

She must leave him, and soon. Her first step must be to effect the separation she knew to be inevitable. At some point, depending on the extent of Marsh's recalcitrance, a divorce would follow. In the meantime Anna would muster the courage she had left, and start a new life for herself—and for her baby.

For a brief, pained instant she pondered the tragic fate of the marriage which had once promised such a happy future. Deep within her remained a bond with Marsh which would never be severed. Whatever the bitterness that had overtaken her feelings for him, she would never be able to forget those first days of heady excitement in his company, of boundless confidence in him. It was nearly unbearable to think that her prideful silence about her personal problems had had such catastrophic consequences.

But it had happened. The clock could not be turned back. Marsh's faith in her must indeed have been frail from the outset, if he was able to abandon it so quickly. And perhaps her own pride, which would not allow her to beg him to reconsider his mistrust, indicated a secret lack of commitment on her own part.

In any case, there was no point in lingering over the complexities of it all. They had failed to make a life with each other; it was as simple as that. In future Anna would retain one precious link to her stormy tryst with Marsh Hamilton: the baby she now carried. Nothing could take that away from her.

Or could it?

A great fear blossomed within her, and was answered by the fierce protectiveness of motherhood. She would need money to bring up the child. What about her job at Ariel? How long would it be before her pregnancy forced her to quit? Would Mr Radier allow her to take time off to have the baby, and then return to work? Wouldn't Mr Foucault be confirmed in his suspicions of female employees, and insist on letting Anna go?

How would she find another job? She dared not cite N.T.E.L. as a reference; that career was over. Her current bosses might give her a reference, but would she be able to earn enough to support a child?

And what about Sally? If Anna left Marsh, she would have to take on Sally's tuition payments again. How could she possibly earn enough for both Sally and her baby?

Unless she accepted alimony and child support payments from Marsh. Money to pay for her child. *His* child.

An angry chill shot through her body as she contemplated the ultimate danger. If there was a divorce, wouldn't Marsh demand custody of his child? A child not yet born . . . Marsh was himself a lawyer. Wouldn't he claim that Anna was not capable of supporting the child adequately?

A welter of confused fears threatened to take

possession of her. Wouldn't Marsh cite the false pretences under which she had married him, and characterise her as an unfit mother? A scheming, mercenary woman who had married him for money while hiding the truth about herself . . .

Losing control of her thoughts, she imagined him supporting his claims by producing the damning N.T.E.L. personnel file in a divorce court. She saw herself vainly trying to protest her innocence before a judge, after already having failed to convince her own husband of it. She saw herself attempting to explain why she had never acted to disprove the file's charges, to regain her job, to clear her name . . . Was she not a security risk? A woman who had tried to use her sexual favours in order to avoid prosecution for her crime?

'For heaven's sake,' she stopped herself with an exasperated laugh, 'get control of yourself! These are nightmares, not real possibilities. It will all work out somehow.'

But in her momentary panic she had begun removing some of her clothes from the closet, as though in preparation for a hasty escape from Marsh. And now, as she contemplated the dresses and shirts that hung in his closet, the idea of leaving this apartment did not seem unreasonable. After last night's cruel quarrel and this morning's dramatic news, she needed time to think. Marsh's bitter, scowling presence was hardly conducive to dispassion-ate reflection.

And Marsh himself could certainly benefit from some well-deserved solitude after his lamentable behaviour towards her. Let him think things over as well, she thought. When they had both had time to cool off, she would tell him about her pregnancy, and firmly insist on an equitable solution to their mutual problem.

Her overnight bag was already filled. Her winter coat lay on the bed beside it. She had moved with a sort of nervous automatism in her preparations to leave. After briefly considering calling Sally, she decided against the idea. Better to stick to her policy of leaving Sally's untroubled college life free of her older sister's complex problems.

After a moment's hesitation she dialled her office number at N.T.E.L.

'Debby Johnson, please,' she said into the receiver.

'Just a moment.'

A loud click jangled in Anna's ear.

'Research 4-A.'

'Call for Debby Johnson.'

'This is Debby.'

'Hi,' Anna began uncertainly. 'This is me.'

'Anna! How are you?'

'Fine. Listen, Deb, would it be terribly inconvenient for you if I stayed at your place for a couple of nights? Or even just for tonight?'

'Not at all,' Debby answered brightly. 'I'd love to have you. But are you all right, Anna? You sound upset.'

'I'm fine,' said Anna, a trifle shocked to realise that her anxiety was so palpable. 'I just need to get away for a little while. Marsh and I . . . well, things are not going well. I have to do some thinking, and I can't do it here.'

'All right,' Debby said authoritatively. 'Just relax, Anna. Let me see . . . I'll tell you what. Do you want to meet me down here after work, or would you rather go over to my place right now?'

'Perhaps I should go straight to your apartment,' said Anna, feeling loath to set foot on N.T.E.L.'s premises.

'Okay, why don't you just head right over, and I'll

call the superintendent—he'll let you in. But do me a favour, Anna. Don't go back out once you get there. You sound a little nervous, and my neighbourhood isn't the greatest. Just wait for me to get there, all right?'

'All right,' laughed Anna, touched by her friend's excessive concern. 'I'll see you later. And thanks a million, Debby.'

After what seemed an eternity of stops and starts in the inner city's crowded traffic, Anna's taxi came to a halt before Debby's ancient brick apartment building. The West Side location was a complex bus ride away from the Loop, so Anna had hailed a cab after stopping at her bank to withdraw sufficient funds for a few days on her own. A maze of unfamiliar streets had passed before her tired eyes during the long ride, and to her surprise she found herself nearly lulled to sleep despite the cab's bumpy progress.

Debby's superintendent was waiting for Anna, and even insisted on carrying her bag upstairs. Apparently grateful for someone to talk to, he managed to air his opinions on the city's political and economic woes in the two minutes it took to reach the apartment. Mustering a smile, Anna thanked him for his help and gratefully closed the door.

Now she sat, her emotions drained, among the furnishings she recognised from occasional visits to Debby during her years at N.T.E.L. Debby's knitting basket was on the couch across from the television. Pictures of her parents and brothers stood on a table. A few of the myriad detective novels she devoured each month were scattered here and there. In the middle of the carpet, like a foreign creature standing at sixes and sevens in the midst of all this domesticity, was Anna's overnight bag, draped by her coat.

Listlessly Anna tried to recall the episodes in her past which had been accompanied by the strange, bereft feelings she now experienced in this lonely silence. There was the time she and Sally had gone to stay with an aunt while their parents attended the funeral of a grandparent. There was Anna's first day at summer camp, when she was eleven years old. And her first day at college, in the unfamiliarity of the dorm. Above all she recalled the first day she had sat at the kitchen table in her family's home, knowing that the place would soon be sold and disappear from her life, for now her parents were both dead. How strange the things of the world seem, she reflected, when one's life is at a crossroads. How unfriendly and foreign the carpets, the windows, the furniture.

Yet somehow, with the passage of time, she had always managed to make a place for herself among people and things which gradually took on the warm supportive glow of the familiar. But she could not help wondering whether such accommodation were to be hers again soon. For months now she had seen the few secure reference points in her life shaken by circumstances, and then finally destroyed. What flat, what furnished room lay ahead for her once her inevitable separation from Marsh became a reality? What future home awaited her new baby next summer? At what hospital would she have the baby? Where would she buy its clothes?

Exhaustedly she gave up thinking of practical things. Moving Debby's knitting basket to the floor, she reclined on the couch and stared mutely at the ceiling. One thing was sure: wherever she ended up, she would not be alone. Her baby would be with her. And no matter what struggles lay ahead, she would soon find herself feeding the child, buying it toys, playing with it, in a room somewhere . . .

Boy or girl? she wondered dreamily. The little hands would wave and grasp at her hair, her face, during the first months. The child would coo with pleasure between the crying spells which would be its only way to communicate its needs. She would carry it around the room, rocking it in her arms to soothe its tears away. She would go to a department store to shop for its first winter jacket, a tiny garment made of quilted, shiny material . . .

She had sunk into sleepy reverie when a gentle knock came at the door. Sitting up with a start, she wondered who it could be. Had Debby come home early? Had she lost her key?

Recalling Debby's warnings about the neighbourhood outside, Anna tentatively turned the knob and opened the door enough to see into the hallway. Dark eyes were staring into her own. A shock of wavy hair, tossed by the wintry wind outside, hung over the strong brow. Concern was in the ebony eyes, along with an enigmatic gentleness she could not fathom.

She stepped back in involuntary trepidation. In a trice Marsh had entered the room and closed the door behind him.

Still retreating despite herself, Anna moved towards the couch. The anger and suspicion she felt at his sudden appearance were outweighed by the visceral fear his powerful form evoked.

He was advancing calmly, a curiously friendly and even mischievous look in his eye.

'You're not running away from me, are you?' he smiled.

'No,' she answered shortly, unsure of his meaning. 'How did you know I was here? Why aren't you working?'

'I am working,' he said. 'I've just finished a job, and

I'm touching bases with the people directly concerned with it.'

'I don't understand,' she said, giving him a wide berth as he sat down. 'How could you know I was here?'

'That was a piece of luck,' he said. 'I happened to be standing right next to Debby when your call came. You know, Anna, it's funny. You've never had anything but bad luck from N.T.E.L., but I seem to get my best breaks there. First I bump into a beautiful woman who becomes my wife, and then I'm lucky enough to be standing there when she calls up in search of a place to stay.'

'Debby shouldn't have told you,' Anna frowned. 'I wanted . . . I want some time alone, Marsh.'

'Of course you do,' he said. 'What woman wouldn't want some time away from a husband who didn't have sense enough to put his faith in her? Especially after the poor fool spent weeks making life a hell for her, because of his stupid, stubborn pride?'

'Marsh, what are you saying?' Unnerved by the tenderness of his demeanour, Anna could not suppress the reflexive suspicion produced by her many angry days with him. 'I don't understand you.'

'What I'm trying to say,' he smiled, 'is that since the day I met you, Anna. I've been the luckiest man in the world, and too damned stubborn to appreciate the fact. If you're willing to listen to me, I hope I can convince you that I'm not all bad.'

'If you're talking about last night,' Anna said coldly, 'you might as well save your breath, Marsh. What happened wasn't the end of the world. I didn't leave home today because of one quarrel, but because . . .'

'I know,' he interrupted, 'I know, Anna. Maybe you should have walked out on me weeks ago. I'm just happy you hung on as long as you did. It shows that you had something left for me inside you. If it isn't too late, perhaps you'll be willing to take a chance on me—on us—one more time.'

'Nothing has changed,' she protested, determined to find out what was behind his apparent change of heart.

'That's where you're wrong,' he corrected. 'Everything has changed. I've changed, Anna. Why, you'd be amazed at how many things can change in one morning. For instance,' he said with a wry grin, 'there's a fellow over at N.T.E.L. named Porter Deman who's out of a job today. I'm sure that was the last thing in the world he expected to happen.'

Anna started involuntarily at his mention of the name she thought he had never heard.

'Porter Deman?' she repeated confusedly. 'How did you . . .'

'And,' he smiled with the complacency of the cat who had eaten the canary, 'you have an unlikely friend to thank for getting Mr Deman his walking papers. Can you guess who?'

She shook her head, dumbfounded by his revelations.

'A lady named May Reynolds,' he grinned.

Anna stared at him with a perplexity in which a first tiny hint of confidence glimmered.

'May?' she said. 'What do you mean? What happened? What are you saying?'

'Before I go on,' he laughed, taking her hand, 'I want to know if you're going to sit here quietly and listen to me, and not jump up and run away without hearing the facts. If you don't mind a small reproach, Anna, I think your trouble all along has been your tendency to go off alone with your problems, instead of asking yourself who your real friends are. Now, will you trust me long enough to listen?'

She nodded uncertainly, feeling a stir of renewed faith under the chaos of her emotions.

'Actually, Anna,' Marsh began, 'I can't blame you all that much for the secretiveness that's brought on your troubles. I'm not an ogre, you know—though I may have acted like one all this time. I can understand what sexual harassment can do to a person. Of course the shock would be terrible, and you would want to forget it at all costs. But hiding the truth from those you love has its own high price, you know.'

'What have you done?' she asked. 'How did you find out . . .?'

'Well,' he said, 'I certainly didn't get the help I needed from you, did I? It took me a while to get my sanity back, after seeing that damned file, and since you wouldn't tell me Deman's name I had to find out for myself. Now that I look back on it all, I can see that you were afraid of what I'd do to that worm if you told me. I have to admit you were right. I was so angry at him—whoever he was—and what he'd done to you, that I let my anger spill over on to you. I should have realised that you would tell me the story in your own time, but instead I blamed you for not trusting me with it from the beginning. I was wrong, Anna, and I apologise.'

As he spoke, the firm lines of his face softened, and Anna began to recognise in him the brightly introspective man she had found so irresistible during the first days of their relationship.

'And,' he sighed, 'the whole story was so outrageous that I'll confess I had my doubts about your complete innocence. There's no point in apologising for that, because it's unforgivable. I had my nerve to doubt you, when I was so outraged that you didn't trust *me* enough to tell me the truth in the first place.'

'It wasn't a question of trust,' Anna explained. 'It

was . . . shame, and embarrassment, and I don't know what else. I should have told you, Marsh. But at the time, I didn't know what was in that file. I just knew that he'd done something . . .'

'I know,' he said. 'I understand, Anna—although I didn't at first. Being as stubborn as you are, I had to figure things out in my own way and in my own time.

'After our quarrel about the file,' he went on, 'I couldn't forget your reasons for not suing N.T.E.L. to get your job back. The only way to do justice to you, on the assumption that you were innocent, was to get the guy who framed you. In order to do that I first had to know who he was. So I made a call to the lady whose apartment we're now sitting in. She told me the whole story: Porter Deman, you, Barbara what's-her-name, Charles Robbins. She didn't know the details about the classified file you were supposed to have pulled from the computer, but she damned well knew the real reason they fired you.'

He smiled, his large hand grazing Anna's cheek.

'I had a lot of male instincts to keep under control,' he confessed, 'and it wasn't easy. But I've had some experience in this kind of thing, so I came up with a plan to get at the truth behind your file. It was pretty simple—the oldest trick in the book, as a matter of fact. Good old May Reynolds, who, as I told you, doesn't happen to be my type—but who is a crackerjack professional and a good-looking woman— went over to N.T.E.L. and got herself a job in your department. This was after I had a little interview with the head of Personnel, Mr Robbins, who had already been contacted by me, and was only too happy to oblige me.'

Placing a finger under her chin, Marsh tilted Anna's face towards his own and grinned with rueful humour.

'Poor Anna,' he said. 'You really haven't had much

luck with men recently. Chuck Robbins is a nice guy, and he was terribly guilty about letting you go. He'd suspected there was something in your story, but hadn't bothered to investigate it thoroughly. When I had his secretary print out your personnel file, he nearly had a heart attack. Of course he could see the malice behind it, so he knew he'd made a big mistake.'

'Was all this the reason why he didn't answer me when I sent him the copy you'd ordered?' asked Anna. 'I never forgave him for that, you know.'

'For that, you can forgive him,' Marsh nodded. 'He was protecting our operation, which had to be secret. For the rest, Anna—for not believing you in the first place, and for not investigating Deman himself—you can forgive him if you have a charitable heart. He was scared to rock the boat, I suppose. Of course, once he'd seen the doctored personnel file and talked to me, he had no choice but to go along with us.

'So,' Marsh continued with a deep breath, 'May, under an assumed name, and dressed in her sexiest outfit, went to work at N.T.E.L. Before a few days had passed, the inevitable happened. Deman cornered her in a back room and told her she'd better have dinner with him, or else. She refused, politely. The next day it was the same thing, only he put the screws to her a little more—dinner with me, or you're fired. Fearfully, May accepted the invitation. At dinner, he put his cards on the table. A good personal relationship is the key to a good working relationship. And so on. Does that ring a bell?'

Anna nodded, flushing anew under the memory of what she had suffered at the hands of Porter Deman.

'Well, we couldn't stop there,' Marsh went on. 'Heroically, courageously, Miss Karff—that was May's alias—resisted Deman's threats. It went on for several weeks—weeks during which, across town, you and I, both as stubborn as ever, were giving each other the silent treatment.' He paused. 'I'll get around to apologising properly for that later. And to making it up to you somehow, Anna. I acted like a pig, and I'll never forgive myself.'

'Marsh, if only I'd known that you were trying to help me all along,' Anna sighed. 'Why didn't you tell me? Why did we have to go on the way we did?'

'Several reasons,' he sighed. 'There was May's cover to consider, and we still didn't have definitive proof of your innocence. After all, there were no traces of Deman's own hand on the computer, either with the classified file or with your doctored personnel file. But most of all, Anna, I'm afraid it was because our quarrel had escalated itself out of all proportion to the situation. I was still mad about the way you'd hidden things from me, and I was in no mood to let you off the hook until I had the goods on Deman. When you sent that file back to Robbins without telling me, it seemed that you were determined to go on keeping your secrets. And last but not least,' he frowned, 'was your new job at Ariel. I couldn't help thinking you were planning to walk out on me as soon as you'd made enough money. Was I wrong, Anna?'

She shook her head in chagrin. 'I'm afraid not,' she admitted. In retrospect she realised she had given Marsh ample reason to fear that her commitment to him was fragile indeed. And now she recalled the probing intimacy of his lovemaking during these unhappy weeks. Her own tormented emotions had blinded her to the wellsprings of affection and commitment his touch had communicated, in spite of his anger.

'Well,' he returned to his story, 'Deman used all his wiles to try to cajole and threaten young Miss Karff into giving him what he wanted. He's really an

eloquent man, in a grotesque sort of way—a born
blackmailer. What he didn't realise was that every one
of his finely turned phrases was going right through
the mike in May's bra and into a tape machine at an
office across the street.' He laughed. 'Some of those
nights when I was working late were quite entertaining.
Well, Miss Karff refused and refused, taking pains not
to be too alluring in her demeanour, so that no one
could accuse her—us—of entrapment. Finally, Deman
resorted to the tactics he had used against you.
"You've had it, Miss Karff, you're finished at
N.T.E.L. I'll get you fired and no one will believe
you," and so on. That was this week.'

He shook his head. 'The man is certainly clever,' he
admitted. 'He didn't want to frame her in the same
way he'd done it to you—too obvious. So he went for
the simplest solution. He decided that Miss Karff had
stolen a letter from his files.

'Today was the red letter day,' he concluded.
'Deman showed up in Chuck Robbins' office, the so-
called stolen letter in his hand. He said he'd found it
in Miss Karff's desk. Without a word, Chuck handed
him his resignation. He told me later this morning that
the look on Deman's face was worth writing home
about. Naturally he demanded an explanation. Chuck
pulled out a cassette, turned on the tape recorder, and
there was good old Porter Deman, explaining to poor
Miss Karff that since she hadn't seen fit to let him
have his way with her, he would see she lost her job.'

Marsh laughed contemptuously. 'Deman, of course,
claimed the girl was a misfit, a scheming seductress
who'd entrapped him. Chuck told him who she really
was, and then pulled out a deposition made by Barbara
what's-her-name—Moore, isn't it?—testifying to what
Deman had done to her. Then, for the *coup de grâce*,
he simply handed Deman a copy of your doctored

personnel file. Well, that did it. Porter signed the resignation. Of course, there's a law against sexual harassment, and the indictment has already been handed down.'

'I can't believe it,' sighed Anna.

'That we got him?' Marsh asked.

'I thought he'd never be stopped.'

'All things are possible,' Marsh smiled, 'when people work together, Anna. When they trust each other. I guess you and I both had to learn that the hard way.'

'Marsh, I don't know what to say,' said Anna. 'When I told Mr Robbins the truth in the first place, and lost my job anyway, I thought the battle was lost. If I'd told you everything then . . .'

'But you hardly knew me, remember?' He grinned, shaking his head. 'I've had a lot of time to think this over, Anna, and it seems to me you weren't at fault. You had plenty of evidence that the system didn't work for victims like yourself. Why fight a losing battle? Even May and I, as lawyers, had to force the corporation to recognise its mistakes. And you're not a lawyer. Your discouragement was perfectly justified.

'But,' he added, his powerful hand resting gently on her shoulder, 'I have my lucky stars to thank for the fact that you felt you knew me well enough to marry me. Although I imagine you've had more than one occasion to think that was a mistake, too.'

Anna shook her head. 'No,' she said. 'I regretted what was happening, and I did think we would have to separate, but I never felt it was a mistake from the beginning.'

'I had a feeling you still had some faith in me,' he smiled, 'since you didn't walk out on me when you had ample reason to. Until today, that is.'

Anna pondered the new light thrown on the past by his revelations. Clearly, the slender thread of commit-

ment binding her to Marsh had weathered many a
storm without breaking.

'I wasn't leaving you for ever when I came here
today,' she said. 'I needed time to think, Marsh.'

'I don't blame you,' he agreed. 'There was a lot to
think about. I hope you don't blame Debby too much
for telling me you'd be here. And by the way,' he
added, 'she explained to me about last night's comedy
of errors. You were apparently so upset at seeing me
in that lounge with May that you didn't notice that
Debby was even more flabbergasted. After all, she
only knew May as Miss Karff from N.T.E.L., and she
was wondering how in hell I knew the girl. But Debby
is a smart woman. She had an inkling of the truth
right away.'

Anna sighed deeply. 'This is all too much,' she said.
'Too good to be true.'

'But it is true,' he murmured, taking her gently in
his strong arms. 'It's all over, Anna. You've had a
tough time, you've been abused and insulted. And,
I'm sorry to say, you didn't have the benefit of the
support I could have given you.'

He kissed her forehead, her hair, with a delicate
tenderness whose tinge of regret underlined the
sincerity of his words.

'I was so crazy about you,' he said, 'from the first
moment you bumped into me outside those elevators,
that I must have been scared of my own feelings. I was
used to handling life on my own, and I suddenly
realised that from that day on I couldn't live without
you. I've tried to hide from it, but it's as true today as
it was then, Anna. I love you.'

At last, after weeks and months of increasing
despair, Anna began to feel the familiar warmth she
had nearly forgotten. Was it possible? Could she be at
home at last in his arms?

'I'm glad you didn't give up on me,' she sighed.

'The feeling is mutual,' he smiled. 'Although I must say I was a little worried today.'

Suddenly Anna recalled the emotions that had driven her from his apartment this morning.

'Anyway,' Marsh was saying, 'it's all in the past now, and I dare to hope that we'll finally be able to invest some confidence in each other. Porter Deman is out of a job, and Charles Robbins is waiting for you to call. He wants you to come back and take over the department, and he's hoping against hope that you'll accept his apologies. Think you're interested?'

Anna squirmed to her knees on the couch and looked into his eyes with the same glimmering happiness that had bewitched him during their honeymoon.

'I'd need maternity leave,' she smiled.

Marsh gazed at her in shock until the meaning of her words came through to him.

'You mean . . .?'

She nodded. 'There'll be another little person in the Hamilton family before too long. And probably every bit as stubborn as his parents!'

'When did you find out?' he asked.

'Today,' she answered. 'That's why I left. I was at my wits' end, and didn't know what to do. But now I know what to do.'

She kissed him tenderly. His arms encircled her with the special gentleness she thought she had lost for ever.

'Anna,' he whispered, 'let's go home. I could sit here for ever, just telling you how much I love you, but you've had a hard day, and you should rest.'

'Yes, let's go home,' she smiled, her arms resting comfortably around him. 'But I don't feel like resting.'

She felt his lips touch her own. His kiss seemed a

promise, charged with the call of a lifetime of happy hours, beckoning from a sunlit future. Her senses yielded willingly to him, for she knew that the past could no longer trouble this intimate beginning.

The future was now.

Your FREE gift includes

Anne Mather—Born out of Love
Violet Winspear—Time of the Temptress
Charlotte Lamb—Man's World
Sally Wentworth—Say Hello to Yesterday